SIDE PLEASE

EIGHT DAYS OF MUMBAI MADNESS

MADAN MOHAN

ISBN
Paperback 979-8-89777-297-1
Hardcase 979-8-89906-302-2

Dedicated to
my dearest aunt
Vasumathy.

2nd September

The train's horn rang out. As it approached the platform, the horns grew louder. And he ran harder and harder, doing everything he could to get there in time to board the train.

He spied a generously endowed middled aged chap standing squarely in his way. He requested loudly, "Side please!" as he rushed along a trajectory bound for a head-on collision with the chap. The chap fortunately did hear and heed his warning and managed to weave away from his path.

Two big strides and he reached the platform and breathed a sigh of relief.

The horn rang again, now much louder. He turned to watch the train's arrival so as to prepare for the leap. It was then, to his horror, that he noticed he was standing right in the train's path. He was not on the platform but the track and the train seemed to be less than a second away from hitting him. It also didn't seem to be slowing down nearly enough to come to a stop before it hit him.

Shailesh panicked. This made no sense. How could this happen? He had been running on the platform surface. He was sure of it. And yet…

He screamed and…sat up on his bed! It was the alarm, not a train horn. This had been a dream and now he had been awakened to the nightmare that lay ahead. Another day of 'side please', another torturous commute!

Why the daily mobile phone alarm had to be the messenger of death, he had no idea. He totally empathized with Farokh Sheikh in the film *Gaman* singing, "*Is Sheher Mein Har Shaks Pareshaan Sa Kyon Hai?*"

Shailesh, a Chartered Accountant, living with his parents at Sapna Kunj, Mulund (an Eastern suburb of Mumbai) had to reach his office using the famed Mumbai local. Mulund- Kurla by local train and then by bus from Kurla station to BKC. Like millions of passengers using the local daily, he had to run, jump and do all it takes with various "Side Please "requests to strangers on his way to somehow get into the jam-packed crowd in the local and likewise somehow alight at Kurla. More often than not, he had to jump in and out of the train before it actually halted. *Jaan ki baazi* (life threat) so as to meet the office meeting deadline! Sigh! You couldn't be anything other than *pareshaan* (harried) in this city.

He trudged out of bed and dragged himself to the washroom. He needed to answer nature's call. In the meantime, his mother would have prepared tea for him. She somehow seemed to rise and sleep with the body clock; it had never let her down all these years. Today as well, she was already awake; the lights in the kitchen indicated as much.

A few minutes later, he got out of the washroom.

He seated himself on a chair by the dining table in the living room.

Mother immediately walked in with a tumbler of tea.

"Good morning, da. Did you sleep well?"

He mumbled a 'good morning' and nodded.

She asked, "Did you brush your teeth?"

He nodded again, not feeling motivated to verbalize his answer.

He knew she meant well. Nay, she meant the best for him. But he still founds questions like these irritating.

He slowly slipped the hot tea and scrolled up and down on his phone screen. He stopped at something that made him laugh rather loudly.

"What is it?" Mother asked.

He pointed to a news article he had opened on the phone browser. The article mentioned BMC's solemn promise to fill up all potholes in the next 24 hours.

She shrugged. "Nothing new."

"Exactly!" He said. "They promise this every year. And every year, they fail. Every year, there are only more potholes than last year."

She didn't seem to find it nearly as amusing as he had.

Mother, a tall, fair complexioned, spare lady with specs, had the brain of a mathematician and the heart of the utterly compassionate. So logical in her thinking and yet her heart beat not for the capitalist but for the poor, the underprivileged. Servants working at their home were a happy lot. She would do 50 % of their work daily and still play the agony aunt not just to them, but to her middle-class neighbours. The snootier set steered clear of her as she wouldn't join their kitty parties.

She jealously guarded her time, rationing it out only for useful tasks. She was B. Com pass but without her tigress skills in Accounting, Shailesh would have had a much tougher time clearing his CA exams.

But, after he had cleared CA, there had been a subtle change in their relationship. He was now the corporate kid who could teach his mother a thing or two but she, as ever, contested him using her robust common sense and sharp intellect. Well, it certainly kept him on his toes.

He knew his father would have laughed out just as loudly as he had. But father was away in Europe on a work trip. He wouldn't be back until the weekend. Oh well!

Father: ex-Army, tall, well built, sharp features with penetrating eyes that could turn jovial or stern depending on the situation. A firm jaw line with a handlebar moustache (of which he was inordinately proud, like the Agatha Christie detective Hercule Poirot) and a sharp chin completed the face. The voice was generally baritone but could purr like Mohd Rafi when speaking to his superior or to them at home when he thought persuasion would work better than a command.

Shailesh finished tea and headed to the bath. In and out in a few minutes.

His mother often wondered aloud whether he had even bathed at all. Not this time.

He browsed through the newspaper quickly as he waited for mother to lay breakfast on the table.

In a few minutes, came the call, "Dei, come, breakfast is ready."

He looked around. Of course, father wasn't there. He was so, so far away in Europe. Father always wanted the newspaper to be neatly folded and put back in as-good-as-new condition for the next person who wanted to read. Shailesh hardly had the patience for all that. He folded it in haphazard fashion and rushed to the table.

He took one look at the breakfast spread for the day and groaned. *Poha*! He didn't mind the taste of it. But it just took too long to eat. Try to hurry up and the tiny little bits would get stuck in the throat. Aargh! Not today of all days when he needed to be in office by 9.30 for the meeting.

"Ma!" He moaned, "Why did you make *poha*?"

"Why dear, what happened?"

"I needed to leave early today. It will take too long to finish the *poha*."

"Oh!" Her agony was genuine and earnest. "You could have told me."

"You never make *poha* on Mondays. It's always *dosa*."

"Well, I thought it would be a change. You like *poha* anyway."

"At least tell me before you change the routine."

"Well, you could just get up early if you need to leave early." She said it gently and in an even-handed tone. She wasn't one for confrontation, never had been. But this was the signal to Shailesh that he had pushed it far enough.

He fell silent and forced himself to finish the *poha* about as fast as he could. Which still took a long time, longer than he needed it to be.

Having finished, he now got dressed in a hurry, slipped on the shoes, wore the backpack on his back and rushed out.

As he alighted the stairs from his first floor flat, he noticed the paint peeling off…and hints of seepage in the wall along the landing too. This building badly needed expenditure on upkeep. But nobody would fork out a penny. Everybody was too hard up to do so, even when they had money to buy themselves a swanky new car. Maybe the building's name was apt after all – Sapna Kunj. An abode where everybody was too busy dreaming!

As he approached the gate of the compound, he looked frantically for any autorickshaw in the vicinity. But he found none.

He kept walking, with his ever-quickening steps approaching a sprint, on towards LBS Marg. There was no other option, even though it would take a good 10 minutes.

As he was doing so, the normally annoying sound of an autorickshaw's engine hit his ears like sweet music. He turned around and yes, an auto was approaching.

He stuck out an arm in the accepted gesture to ask motorists, specifically autos, to stop.

The auto came to a stop next to him and the driver asked, " 'Tation?" In Mumbai lingo, the 's' was always silent in station. Again, an auto headed to the railway station was exactly what Shailesh needed.

Just to be sure, he confirmed, "Mulund."

The driver turned his head and looked at the passenger seat quickly. That was the Mumbai autowala's way of indicating that you could get in.

And so Shailesh did.

Luckily, the traffic wasn't too bad and in five minutes, the driver had reached the station.

Shailesh stepped out and offered a 20 rupee note.

The driver raised his eyebrows as if to ask Shailesh about the 1 rupee deficit.

Shailesh said he didn't have change and offered another 10 rupees note.

The driver asked, "Where do I go for nine rupees change? Do you think I am mad?"

Shailesh asked, "Then, can I gpay the amount to you?"

The driver glared angrily at him. "Leave it, keep your precious 1 rupee." And with that, he turned the vehicle away.

Shailesh shrugged. This really was much ado about nothing.

He had bigger fish to fry.

He rushed to the staircase to get to platform no.2. He hoped the fast train hadn't already departed.

He looked at the indicators and they confirmed that it was yet to arrive but barely a minute away.

He shot up the stairs like a rocket headed for the stars.

A young man and a young woman were drifting across the breadth of the staircase as they held each other's hands. It was a romantic enough sight but it alarmed Shailesh and he yelled, "Side please!" as he approached.

The dude scowled as he turned inward towards his romantic interest to make way for Shailesh.

Shailesh had no time for explanations nor apologies. He reached the top of the stairs, got to the one taking him to platform no.2 and started the descent. The train was already at the other end of the platform and about to march in. But he had got this now. He could make it to the platform before the train came to a stop. He had done this many times before and would surely do it again.

And then, just at that moment, an army of fish selling women began their climb up the stairs, three of them shoulder to shoulder. There would be no asking them to 'side please'. He quickly hedged to the left corner of the staircase and continued his sprint. God, how he wished he could have been Jackie Chan from Rush Hour and just fly over the heads of those fish ladies to get to the platform!

He made it to the platform but there was yet work to do. The first compartment was reserved for ladies and the second one was, well, second class. He *could* get into that one as a last resort but his first preference would be to make it to the third compartment and get into the first class section.

By now, the train had arrived and the usual bout of organized chaos had been unleashed as people jostled to either get in or get out. More of the former. This was rush hour and Mulund wasn't the biggest magnet for workers. But the flow was still two way and the platform wasn't nearly big enough to accommodate all this movement.

Thinking quickly, Shailesh decided to get into the second compartment. After all, second class was only slightly more crowded than first class.

He hoped, though…nah, one look and his hopes were dashed. The *bhajan mandali* was very much in attendance. There was just a pause as the esteemed singer helped himself to a few sips of water to preserve his golden throat. He would soon go forth and unleash with percussionists in consort.

Onboard Mumbai's local trains, especially in the second class compartments, every inch of space was precious. A fourth seat was created in seating for three. People stood in the space between two opposing rows of seats. The corner row offering seating for seven commuters usually seated at least eight, sometimes nine. Every inch of space was bitterly contested and optimally utilized…except the space reserved for the *bhajan mandali*. These esteemed musicians were given all the comfort they needed to be able to freely practice their trade…and regale their fellow commuters.

Shailesh dreaded the journey even as the train had only just started to ease out of the station. He knew he would have a splitting headache from enduring this, ahem, entertainment by the time he got down at Kurla. He had no choice. He couldn't have afforded to miss this train to be in office on time.

The train had only one halt en route – Ghatkopar. But he hoped it would not resort to that which fast trains plying on the Mumbai suburban rail network were infamous for – halts between stations! There was a traffic jam of sorts on the railway tracks and up in the skies and on the airport runway. These just happened to be more organized and disciplined jams unlike the sheer chaos on the roads. With trains running with only three minutes of headway between each other, it took very little to cause minor delays. But the Mumbai commuter always planned his commute 'cut-to-cut' — organizing a schedule that required a precision that the city couldn't always live up to, in fact frequently didn't live up to.

And so, delays that could hardly be considered extraordinary would still be enough to foil Shailesh's masterful plan to reach office on time.

He was fortunate again. The train only stopped at Ghatkopar and then whistled past Vidyavihar. He moved towards the doorway on the right-hand side of the compartment. He appreciated this aspect of Kurla station, if nothing else. Fast trains bound for CSMT always stopped at platform no.6 and slow trains at platform no.4. There would be no last minute change of platform necessitating a stampede to the other doorway. Small mercies these were, when you considered what awaited once you got down at Kurla!

He managed to inch up to the edge of the doorway, positioning himself perfectly to get down before the train had come to a stop. This was necessary if he was to have any chance of avoiding a slow crawl up the staircase at platform no.6.

The train eased into the platform and slowed down. He prepared to get down. He was almost beaming. Today was turning out to be a perfect day, barring the *bhajan mandali*-induced headache.

And then…he moaned, loud enough to cause some fellow commuters to turn and look at him. It was the sight of a train pulling into platform no.5. Any hopes of a smooth passage up the staircase were now dashed.

Sure enough, even before the train could slow down enough where he could get down without landing teeth first on the floor, the staircase was already milling with people. He resigned himself to fate and lost interest.

But his fellow commuters lined up behind him hadn't. They started restlessly imploring him to get down. At last, when it was still about ten feet away from the dead stop, he got down and rushed to the staircase. Good thing that he had, for had he slowed down upon alighting, he would have faced angry stares and shakes of the head from fellow commuters…for not getting down fast enough from the moving train.

As it was, he still heard somebody say within earshot, "Everyday, there's someone like this."

Without turning around, he said aloud, "Because we are not Shaktimaan like you."

If the other person had wanted to rush forth and take it up with him, it was too late. They had both joined the crowd crawling up the staircase. There was nothing to do for the next couple or more minutes until you got to the summit. It was a forced détente.

After he got to the top, he dashed ahead, partly to thwart any possibility of the other guy picking up a fight and partly because he had a bus to catch. To be precise, BEST bus route no. 310. Originating at Kurla station (West), it terminated at Bandra Terminus. More importantly, it passed through Bandra Kurla Complex. Or BKC as everybody in Mumbai called it.

Shailesh often wondered about this West/East business in Mumbai. Why did they say Kurla (West) or Kurla (East)? Was it unique to the city? It might well be. For he had been to Chennai many times to visit his aunt and had never noticed anybody refer to West or East of the same locality with reference to which side of the railway tracks they lay on except maybe one or two. But then, Mumbai was also quite unique in transporting the equivalent of a megapolis on its local trains every day. It was also an impossible ordeal were you to land up on the wrong side of the tracks in Mumbai, unlike Chennai!

Presently, he raced down the stairs at Platform no.1 and made his way to the exit.

Lo and behold, there was Bus no.310. As he dashed towards it, he heard the engine roar. It was about to start. If he had had wings, he would have flown up to it. As it was, he yelled out loudly in Marathi, begging it to stop. Standees at the rear door heard him and informed the conductor. The conductor dragged the rope running top left along the length of the bus for a single ring. It indicated to the driver to stop. And so, just as the bus inched forward a little, it stopped.

He put Usain Bolt to shame as he went through the last three steps to get to the rear door. He boarded and profusely thanked those standees as well as the conductor. The conductor nodded gruffly while the standees accepted his thanks with big smiles on their faces. The bus was full, so it would be another long, standing journey. He had no choice. The meeting.

The ride through Kurla wasn't remotely as smooth as the train journey. This was only to be expected. Monday morning madness at Kurla market was unavoidable, especially with steady, if not overwhelming, rain like today. He could abide by the traffic but the odours, oh dear! All at once, a whole variety of odours hit him and hit him hard. That was Kurla. Scents (*if* they could be called *that*) that you didn't know existed would assault you. This wasn't unique to Kurla. Mumbai as such was, er, an exhibition of odious wonders. But in Kurla, everything kind of came together in a way it didn't elsewhere in the city. The dangerously crowded staircases at the station, the incredible gridlock on the roads, the cacophonous noise in Kurla market, the smells, the filth, every essence of Mumbai amplified to 11. If Mumbai were a symphony, then Kurla would be its crescendo. If you could handle Kurla, you could handle anything Mumbai threw at you. And he had been handling Kurla for a long time. He didn't like it, but he handled it all the same. For every Mumbaikar living in the Eastern Suburbs and working in BKC, Kurla was a daily rite of passage.

Check that, there was something all these years of passing through Kurla hadn't taught him to handle and that was the noise. Not that the noise was specific to Kurla in any way but…it was deafening all the same.

A kerfuffle on the roads reminded him of this noise attack he so wished he could run away from. A car parked on the left had taken off and cut sharply to the right as the driver needed to make a right turn. But an impatient autowala had pushed ahead and cut into his way before he could do so. And before the autowala could find his way, another car, this one from the opposite side of the road wanted to turn right. And now, as the three vehicles finding themselves locked honked incessantly imploring the other to move, the traffic had ground to a halt, unleashing in turn an even louder cacophony of horns. In the midst of this, harried pedestrians squeezed past the stranded vehicles, trying their best to contract their bodies to avoid colliding into each other.

And then, just like that, the car managed to turn right, the autowala proceeded straight ahead and the other car completed its own right turn too. The bus moved again and Shailesh exhaled loudly.

Half an hour later, he finally reached his bus stop. His office block was just behind the bus stop. No further roadblocks. He consulted his watch. It was two minutes past 9:30. He shook his head. Ajay sir would be fuming. Sweaty and a little dishevelled, he continued his dash towards the office.

As he approached the gate, though, a bike passed close to the sidewalk and through a large puddle of water. He happened to be passing close to the puddle at that very instant and the splash…found itself very much at home on his pristine white shirt.

As he stared at the mess, he felt something land on his shirt pocket. With dread, he took one look and it was exactly what he had feared it would be. The droppings of a crow perched on the tree above.

In an instant, Mumbai had taken something from him in exchange for the near-perfect commute.

With perfect timing, another pedestrian passed him by, enjoying a Hindi film song on his phone. He heard Mohd Rafi sing the words, "*Zara Hatke Zara Bachke Yeh Hai Bambai Meri Jaan*".

He smiled wryly and dashed towards the office block, pretending nothing had happened.

He walked into the office and quickly made for the restroom to wash off the stain from the crow-dung and rearrange his hair that had been somewhat dishevelled from the train commute.

That done, he walked briskly towards the conference room where the meeting had been scheduled. He gingerly opened the door…only to find the lights were out and there was nobody in.

He turned and looked around the office. He spotted his colleague Kunal, who should have been in the meeting.

He looked at Kunal and pointed to the meeting, gesturing to ask what was up.

Kunal shrugged and smiled.

He mouthed, "Ajay sir."

Kunal pointed to Ajay's cabin. It was vacant.

Shailesh was pissed off. All his Olympian efforts to make it on time had been in vain (not that he *had* made it on time anyway).

He walked up to Kunal. "What shall we do now?"

Kunal said, "*Chal*, let's go get some tea."

"Good idea!"

They went to the tea vending machine in the cafeteria and made themselves a cup each. Mansi, one of the managers, was leaving the cafeteria just then and warmly greeted them.

They then sat down in the cafeteria and sipped through the tea

Shailesh stretched a little and said, "Damn, I really hate working in BKC. When I worked at Lower Parel, I could step outside and get cutting *chai* and vada pav on days like these."

Kunal replied wryly, "Well, I tried having pani puri from a stall the other day and I needed Roko to make it to office the next day."

"Where did you have it?"

"Chowpatty. Girgaum."

"Dude, having *anything* there is dangerous for your stomach."

"So where should I?"

"Come to Mulund. I will treat you to the best pani puri in Mumbai."

"Thanks, but it's such a long way from Grant Road."

"Yeah, I forgot you are a SoBo dude." Shailesh smirked.

Kunal smiled and ignored him.

Kunal grew serious and whispered, "What if he comes while we are here?"

Shailesh quipped wryly, "He will surely call either of us on the phone."

"And he will be angry."

"After himself being late?"

"*Yaar*, you know that's how he is."

"So? We are supposed to stay stationary at our desks and not even fetch tea? Come on, don't be so afraid. Anyway, in that case, let's just finish the tea quickly and not debate this."

They finished drinking tea in a few minutes and returned to their desks.

The clock struck 10. And then, 10.15. At 10.30, Ajay finally walked into his cabin. As soon as he sat down in his office, he called both and told them to sit in the conference room. No explanation for why he had got late was offered.

Ajay rubbed a few remaining strands of hair on his bald head as he settled his equally round body into the chair. In all the time that Shailesh had worked here, once, by accident, he had spied Ajay Sir smiling as he spoke to his wife. Man, he looked so innocent! But, at work, he was Hitler incarnate. Tough, no-nonsense, arbitrary and practically a humanoid! You were lucky if any meeting ended on a cordial note. In fact, such endings brought forth a torrent of abuses the next day, as Ajay Sir felt a compelling need to compensate for the unwanted niceties, so Shailesh and team prayed for meetings to end on a professional but dismissive note!

It was a long, long day at work, mostly thanks to Ajay's tardiness. It wasn't the first time and it wouldn't be the last. Ajay loved to call Monday morning 'sharp' 9.30 meetings and 9 times out of 10, would be late. But because he did very occasionally make the appointed time for those meetings, Shailesh couldn't take the chance of being late himself for these meetings.

They broke for lunch at 1 PM. Ajay usually spent an hour and a half from 1 to 2.30. Half an hour for the lunch, another hour to catch up on the markets and put in trades. It was the one breather during the work day everyone working under him was guaranteed, sort of...except on days the markets were closed but their office wasn't!

Shailesh joined Kunal and Jaideep (who too reported to Ajay) as well as Anup and Mahesh (who both reported to a different manager) as they occupied one table of six at the cafeteria.

Today, Jaideep had with him another colleague.

He said, "Guys, let me introduce you to Narayan."

Everyone said hi which Narayan shyly reciprocated.

Jaideep added, "Narayan has joined from the Pune office."

"Oh!" Kunal asked. "Who were you reporting to?"

"Sanjay."

Shailesh almost spat out the *dal makhni*. "You have left Sanjay sir for...Ajay?"

"Yes." Narayan answered unsurely. And asked. "Why?"

"Well.." Shailesh could hardly muster a response. The others burst out laughing and he joined them.

Narayan said, "I was working with Sanjay for four years. Wanted a change."

"Careful what you wish." Shailesh quipped.

Jaideep interjected, "Guys, guys, you will scare him away. This is his first day in this office."

"And first day in Mumbai?" Kunal asked.

Narayan nodded.

Kunal shrugged. "Well, you'll find out. It's not *all* bad. But…"

Shailesh interjected. "You'll get texts and calls during lunch as Jaideep just did."

Sure enough, Jaideep had got up to answer a call from Ajay. There was usually *one* team member who would get a call during lunchtime from Ajay. He was considerate enough not to disturb everyone every day. But *one* person would have to take one for the team every day, yes.

Shailesh continued, "If you're going to travel by train, getting in and getting out could be challenging."

Kunal added, "And during rains, trains could stop on some days."

Shailesh added, "Rent is also higher than in Pune."

Narayan replied with a smile, "I am staying with my uncle here."

"Good for you." Kunal quipped.

"Oh, and if you choose not to go by train and take a bus instead, your travel time could almost double." It was a one last thing from Shailesh.

Narayan said, half-questioningly, "Mumbai is also a very happening place, right?"

Kunal replied. "Yes, lots of things happening. The other day, the bridge at CSMT collapsed." He added, "But nobody died."

Narayan's face grew pale.

Shailesh worried that Narayan might well seek the safety of Pune ASAP, at which point Jaideep would chew Shailesh and Kunal out.

He assured Narayan, "Don't worry, we're just teasing you. You'll be alright. We are here to help. Welcome to Mumbai."

Narayan smiled weakly. Everything he had heard prior to this had had a ring of truth and this assurance on the other hand had a ring of…emptiness. Well, the deed was done. He would have to find out if he was going to be miserable here or not.

At 6 PM sharp, Mansi turned off the lights in her cabin and left her office. She usually left at or around 6.

Jaideep quipped in a very soft voice to Anup, "I don't remember the last time I saw her put in a nighter."

"Maybe she never did." Anup suggested.

"I guess that's the key to becoming a manager. Never working late."

They had both assumed they were out of earshot but Mansi stopped, turned around and, smiling, said, "You're right, Jaideep. It's probably my time management skills that helped me become a manager. Because when I get home, I will still need to make dinner for Jeevan and Advait. Not to forget my in-laws. And I will have to wash the utensils after that. Then, make breakfast for all as well as lunch for myself, Jeevan and Advait. And then come here, give my all for 9 hours without *sutta* breaks on the hour. Yeah, that's indeed the key to becoming a manager."

Jaideep looked down at the floor, feeling terribly embarrassed.

Embarrassment turned to anger as he heard a few claps of applause. It was Shailesh.

He glared and Shailesh shrugged, chuckled and turned his attention back to the laptop.

At 8PM, Ajay finally pushed off. He stayed in Kalina, only a short drive away. For Shailesh, on the other hand, a long commute awaited.

He was in no mood to wait for 310 to reach Kurla station. Instead, he tried to configure a ride on Ola/Uber from office to station. The wait time was a minimum ten minutes. With a frustrated sigh, he walked out of the office, looking for an auto. He soon spotted one.

He asked, "'Tation?"

The autowala made a weary expression and ran a hand through his hair. He then said, "I need half return."

"Done."

"Hundred one way and half return fifty. 150."

"Boss, that's too much."

"I won't get any passenger from station now. Everyone is returning home."

"120."

"140."

"130."

Again, the autowala ran his hand through his hair. He then looked at his passenger seat. Shailesh exulted lightly and got in.

Twenty minutes later, he had reached the station. He had even overtaken the previous 310 trip en route. The decision to pay an exorbitant fare had been well worth it.

He made straight for platform 1. A slow train would do just fine at this time of day, he thought. But as he looked around at the platform, he realized any train would have to do. There wasn't standing room in the platform. The indicator gave an indication of why. It was getting to half past eight and the 8.12 slow to Thane had yet to arrive. The trains were running horribly late.

He asked around and somebody suggested there had been some overhead fault at Byculla during the evening. While they had fixed things an hour ago, there was still some ways to go to get the trains back on schedule.

By some twist of fate, there was an announcement. The 8.12 was now expected to arrive shortly.

In a couple of minutes, the bright yellow lights of the approaching train pierced the eyes of those looking intently in its direction. The crowd stepped forward an inch collectively and in perfect coordination, even when there wasn't a millimetre of space left.

Shailesh was right at the back of the platform. He didn't think he had a chance. And he was right. As the train stopped, a virtual stampede broke out. Mumbaiites, even ordinarily an impatient sort, got really agitated on days of such extreme delays. And yes, delays exceeding 10-15 minutes during rush hour in Mumbai were extreme. With the trains already packed to the brim, the system couldn't withstand such delays. Somehow, commuters avoided getting into fisticuffs, but it always seemed to get to the brink of that situation.

He let the train go.

In another two minutes, the next train, this one bound for Kalyan, came through. But even the shorter headway didn't help. There were still too many commuters for too little train space. Once again, Shailesh joined the ones who stayed back.

Five minutes later, it was a Badlapur bound train. By now, the competition to get in wasn't so intense. But the trouble was, a Badlapur bound train was already inherently more crowded. With it running late, it was even more crowded.

Shailesh baulked at the prospect. A fellow commuter who waited to get in and stand on the footboard teased him, "Are you waiting for another Thane local?"

He scowled. Well, if he did, so what?

The next one was a Titwala. This time, he decided to get in. It too was crowded. But it was getting late and he was starting to feel hungry. Another commuter asked, "Not waiting for Thane local?"

"Yeah, man, need to get home." Shailesh replied with a wry shake of the head.

"That's the spirit of Mumbai." The other man said and laughed.

"Yes," Shailesh said to himself, "This is what the spirit of Mumbai is about. Waiting for a Thane local that doesn't come and then settling for Titwala when you could have had Badlapur in any case."

Man, that made it sound like deciding which girl he was going to date for the night. Mumbai really did make you romance getting crushed in the trains, he thought.

3rd September

Shailesh got up the day after on his own, before the alarm. Perhaps, the sound of rain had something to do with it. This wasn't what people living in other cities thought of as rain. Other people thought of a pleasant pitter-patter, sometimes surging to a steady downpour. All those a Mumbaiite could handle with ease. Or even torrential rain. No, this was the kind of rain that felt like there had been a breach in the clouds, permitting the sea to unload vertically onto the surface. It was rain so intense it sounded like a constant roar, almost deafening, and blocked your view of just about everything.

Shailesh gingerly got out of bed.

He wasn't super eager to go to work today. But…Ajay sir! Ajay was quite reasonable about sick leave…just so long as you could produce a doctor's prescription to establish your sickness. Mild fevers that didn't require a doctor's intervention also didn't require a day off from work in his expert opinion. But any other kind of sick leave, he was perfectly alright with. But rain leave…now *that*, Ajay simply didn't approve of. The moment an employee asked for leave, Ajay would launch into a rewind capsule of how he had been stranded in office on 26/7 (on 26th July 2005, the city was submerged by a whopping 90 cm of rain!) and stayed at work for two days, keeping the flag flying for the company. The elements were to be braved against, not surrendered to, in his expert opinion.

Shailesh pre-emptively deferred to his expert opinion and decided he would have to get to work somehow. He did, however, decide to check the tide timings. This had lately become a new addition to the daily routine of Mumbaiites during the rainy reason. Along with train timings, they checked the tide timings as well. And sure enough, high tide started at 12 PM today. During high tide, the stormwater drains could not empty out into the sea and heavy rain during that time could lead to waterlogging. If intense rain kept up till then, getting back home could be seriously challenging.

He thought about it for a while and decided to get on with the business of getting ready and watch how the situation developed. This was a time tested Mumbaiite strategy to ace the commute on rainy days. Pretend you were going to work for sure and get ready accordingly. *Not* going to work was an activity that took no time to prepare for.

He also surfed through the Marathi news channels which usually started flashing live updates about the rains and the situation of rail/road mobility right from 6AM or so. The picture they presented wasn't very comforting. The trains were still running but already, water was seen accumulating on the tracks at Kurla.

As he finished up on tea, the rains seemed to ease up in intensity, reducing to a heavy downpour that was no longer savage and destructive.

He had made up his mind. Aloud, he said, "Ma, I am going to office today."

She was alarmed. She left the kitchen and came up to him to ask, "But how will you go, pa? The trains might stop soon."

"I will take the car today."

"But it's raining so heavily."

"It's already slowing down. It will be ok."

"Take care, dear. If the rains don't stop by the afternoon, come back home. Don't take unnecessary risks. You are working for a company, not the army."

"Ajay sir doesn't understand that."

"Maybe if he had actually been in the army, he would." She quipped. Shailesh's father had, after all, been in the army prior to his current senior role in procurement.

"Well, it is what it is." Shailesh said.

Shailesh had his bath and got dressed. Breakfast awaited him at the table. Corn flakes today. Today he didn't mind if it took time. He needed the time to think over whether he was gonna go or not.

As he munched on the flakes, mother asked, "Did you hear anything regarding that Zimbabwe offer?"

Irritated, he said, "It's not an offer, ma. Just a phone call with their HR."

"OK pa. I don't know. I never got to work in an office."

He took a deep breath. He knew he was being unreasonable. He offered a more elaborate explanation, "The HR manager said she would schedule an interview soon. Didn't say when, but mostly on a Saturday."

"That's good. You will be able to attend it."

"Yes, but it means they work Saturdays."

"Hmmm."

"I need to think hard about it. I saw reports saying nobody gets water there and that there are acute petrol shortages. And what about safety?"

"I spoke to Kittu Mama. He has been living there for more than twenty years and said it's very safe."

"Ma, that's Zambia." The old irritation returned.

"And Zambia and Zimbabwe together used to be Rhodesia. Zambia split early, first as Northern Rhodesia, then being renamed as Zambia when it became independent."

For a moment, Shailesh was stunned. Mother couldn't help but flash a satisfied, even slightly smug, smile.

He finally asked, "So…what does that mean?"

"It means that they shared the same culture and you can relate the experience in one country to the other to a large extent."

"Well, can you relate the experience of Pakistan to India?" He counter-questioned.

She slapped her forehead and said, "You just keep arguing constantly. That's the one quality you got most from your father. Do as you wish."

He was irritated again. He thought his was a valid question. Nevertheless, he did need to think about it. For a simple reason. The money was rather good. Anyhow…first, there would be an interview and he would need to make the shortlist.

The rains continued at a steady clip without being menacing as they had been in the early hours of the day. He decided to take a chance. He took the car keys and stepped out.

His car was a Petrol Nexon. He had wanted something that would be compact while offering the ground clearance advantage of an SUV. The Nexon had fitted the bill very well. There were things he didn't entirely like about it, but it was a car he could live with.

He drove out of the compound and towards LBS road. No waterlogging so far.

On to LBS road and he drove South towards Nahur. He turned left at the Sonapur junction to cross over to Mulund East and head to the Eastern Express Highway. Or EEH as the MMRDA or BMC folks called it.

He spotted a newspaper stall at the turning and quickly picked up a Mid Day. He missed Mumbai Mirror with its lovely, Mumbai-centric columns. Afternoon was long dead. At least Mid Day was alive and well. If the gridlock was long enough, he could browse through the pages as he waited. He had had occasion to before!

As he turned and started to merge to the middle, a biker cut in and sped past him, missing him by a whisker. As the biker did so, he gave Shailesh a glare and cussed.

Shailesh did a double take. Had he made a mistake? No! There was no signal for the biker unless he had taken a U turn to go back up the other way on the flyover!

Shailesh shook his head and carried on. He connected his phone via USB to the car speakers and let the music play. He had a playlist of about 25 old Hindi songs on the phone storage. That amounted to about 100 minutes. He thought that would suffice for the commute. In the mornings, it usually *was* enough.

He drove on and found a BEST bus ahead of him. He wanted to overtake the bus, but the driver had strategically positioned the bus in such a way that there wasn't enough room either to the right or the left of the bus to overtake. The driver also put his hand out of the window, forewarning Shailesh against any attempts to overtake. Shailesh obeyed.

In the meantime, the bus arrived at a stop and stopped in that exact neither here-nor-there position. Shailesh was stuck behind it with no option but to wait until either the driver decided to relent and give way or he could finally join the EEH which would be too much road for a lone BEST bus to block!

As he waited for the bus to get a move on, he began to take in the lyrics of the song. It was Kishore

Kumar singing the words, "*Pyar Hamein is Mod Pe Le Aaya*". He sang along, but instead singing, "*Ajay Hamein Is Mod Pe Le Aaya*".

At long last, the bus did move and so could he. But wait, here was an auto swerving violently to the right for no particular reason, just as he had been lining up the overtake. He braked hard, slowing down and allowing both the mad bus and the mad auto to go ahead. Aargh, how he hated driving in Mumbai! Yes, yes, he knew driving was at least equally as maddening, if not even more so, in other Indian metros. He didn't care. If the trains were bad enough to endure, the car driving experience hardly offered any succour in Mumbai

He carried on and soon got to join the EEH. From thereon, it was relatively smooth sailing. He nodded away to his favourite songs and sang along here and there. And then, just as he began to sing along to *Zindagi Aa Raha Hoon Main*, he hit a mega, mega traffic jam at Priyadarshini junction. He sang, "*Traffic Mein Phas Gaya Hoon Main*" and shook his head in frustration.

After inching on half-clutch for 10 minutes, he could finally get a move-on.

He drove on towards Sion and moved to the right lane, ready to climb up the Chunnabatti-BKC flyover. As he approached the mouth of the flyover, a rickety old Premier Padmini (one of the rare privately owned ones still plying on the streets) sped past him from the left and cut in just in time to avoid crashing into the flyover wall. Kishore sang, "*Yeh Kya Hua Kaise Hua.*" Shailesh said wryly, "*Ab Kya Sunaye*" and dragged the USB cable out of the stereo. He had had quite enough of the music. The traffic, really.

Fortunately, from there, there wasn't much further to go. What didn't help was a sudden intensifying of the rain. It started raging against the city again. The sheer force of the downpour was so immense, Shailesh felt it could even sweep away his Nexon. It didn't but visibility was non-existent. He hoped and prayed he would spot the bumper of the car ahead in time to brake.

He managed to carefully negotiate this last rain-filled passage and reach the office parking lot.

As he was driving into a vacant slot, somebody else pulled in, playing music he didn't recognize very loudly, with a male voice humming what sounded like a creepy falsetto to him.

Had he known his Radiohead, he would have recognized the song as *Burn The Witch*.

As it was, he said aloud in Hindi, "Who plays this kind of music, man!" A little too loudly, perhaps, for the one who had played that song, chuckled and shook his head as he locked his car and walked towards the elevator.

Shailesh shrugged and imitated that shake of the head behind his back. Phew, was he relieved to have made it. That last stretch had been super tricky.

But the rain showed no signs of letting up.

At office, he got engrossed with work as Ajay required an urgent deliverable.

But he couldn't take his mind off the weather.

Every half an hour or so, he would get up from his seat and go over to the window by the xerox machine area to take a quick peek at the rain and the streets.

The third time that he did so, Ajay stepped out of his cabin and barked, "Shailesh, what's happening to the deliverable?"

"I am working on it, sir." He offered.

"Then go back to your desk and work on it." Ajay thundered.

And so, Shailesh was unable to even carry out his weather check. Consequently, he ended up forgetting about it.

Until, at 12.30, Mahesh came by his desk.

Mahesh whispered, "What's your plan, boss? Can you drop me to Airoli?"

"Plan? Meaning?"

"Boss, there is already some waterlogging. Not much but it's high tide now. And it's still raining heavily."

"Man….got a deliverable."

"Ajay?"

Shailesh nodded and Mahesh instantly grimaced.

Shailesh offered, "I will be done in the next five minutes. Let me email it to him and then ask."

"If you ask, he's never going to give permission."

"Gotta try. Besides, going without asking him would be suicidal."

Shailesh wrapped up the presentation, emailed it and waited a couple of minutes.

Ajay called on his extension and asked to see him.

He went in.

Ajay looked as if in a surprisingly good mood. He said, "I think this is fine. If at all any changes need to be made, I will do them myself."

"Ok sir."

"Right…you can go."

"Uh…sir, there was one more thing."

Ajay was puzzled. "What?"

"Sir, it's already getting waterlogged and high tide started more than an hour ago."

"Ok. And?"

"Sir, I will need to leave now otherwise it will get unsafe."

"Dude, if it is that unsafe, why bother to come to work? Stay at home, na?"

"Sir, I have finished the deliverable and I will keep tracking and replying to emails."

"That's not the point. You are paid to work 9.30 to 6."

"I work longer than that anyway, sir."

Ajay shrugged dismissively, "I haven't seen it. Work from home (making a gesture to indicate quotes) doesn't count."

Just as Shailesh was wondering what he could say to Ajay to win him over, Ajay's phone rang.

It was Ajay's wife. Now…Ajay kept the volume on maximum on the phone and his wife tended to speak very loudly on phone calls. So, what she said was usually audible to anybody else in Ajay's vicinity even when Ajay hadn't turned on the speaker.

She asked in Marathi, "Baba, when are you coming home? Come quickly. Water is already accumulating. How many times should I tell you?"

Ajay turned away from his instrument and looked at Shailesh, who was beaming, with a scowl on his face.

He mouthed, "Go!"

Whether he had meant to say he wanted Shailesh out of the room or out of the office, he didn't specify. But Shailesh was one to take his chances. He smiled at Mahesh and asked him to get ready.

Kunal looked at them as they were leaving and asked, "He let you go?"

"He had to. His missus asked him to come back ASAP."

Kunal suppressed a laugh and made a thumbs up expression to them.

They dashed towards the car. There was a let up in the rains and they needed to take this chance before the rains returned and the waterlogging made it impossible to drive.

Shailesh turned onto the road out of the parking lot. He soon merged with the main road and proceeded to Chunnabatti flyover. There was waterlogging right away. Barely ankle deep but enough to slow down the traffic. The vehicles – his and the ones ahead – crawled as they safely negotiated this stretch.

Mahesh said, worried, "It's already so bad. What are we going to do?"

Shailesh was super-relaxed. "This is nothing, re. We will make it easily if this is how bad it's going to get."

Getting out of the waterlogged stretch, they accelerated hard for the flyover.

Perhaps not hard enough because the owner of the SUV behind Shailesh honked multiple times and then swerved to the right to overtake him.

Shailesh quipped, "It's always the SUV guys who are so impatient. Bullies!"

Mahesh said, "Nothing like that, man, my father drives an Alto and he gets impatient too."

Shailesh shrugged. "Well, different strokes, I guess. And what about you?"

Mahesh shook his head vigorously. "I don't drive."

They got down from the flyover. More waterlogging on the Sion-Panvel highway (of which one arm took a slight right at Priyadarshini to become VN Purav Marg and the other proceeded straight on to become the EEH). Not very deep, again, but enough to slow down the traffic.

Mahesh asked, "Boss, will we make it?"

Shailesh replied, "Yeah, yeah, we will. Don't worry. This car has good ground clearance."

Just then, an auto rickshaw ahead of him suddenly sputtered to a stop. He swerved hard to the left and avoided it but due to the water logging, the car wasn't quite in control. He managed the manoeuvre without dangerous oversteer.

But Mahesh panicked and screamed, "Take care, man, you almost hit him."

Just then, a bus cut in sharply from the left and overtook Shailesh's Nexon. As it did so, its rear nearly hit the Nexon. This time, with right of way available on the right, Shailesh swerved quickly to the right to avert the collision. Once again, the car skidded and got perilously close to the divider. And yet again, Shailesh managed to adjust the car into position before any such thing happened.

But not before Mahesh panicked again, "See, again, we nearly had an accident."

Shailesh was annoyed. He slowed the car down drastically and put on the emergency lights.

He then gestured to Mahesh and said, "Here, all yours."

Mahesh grew red-faced. "Shailesh, what are you doing? I can't drive."

"Then please allow me to and stop your backseat driving."

"Well, I am sitting in the front alongside you."

"Whatever. You have no idea how difficult it is to drive in these conditions. So let me concentrate. Don't worry, I have handled this kind of weather before. We will get out safely. Just please stop panicking."

"Ok, ok." Mahesh said in a huff.

But as they headed past the Priyadarshini signal, the rain picked up again, dramatically so. The skies were roaring angrily again, as if lashing out at the wanton neglect of the environment in the city. Had they known that even getting marooned wouldn't get the powers-that-be to pause, they might not have bothered.

The force of the rain was such that, together with the lack of run-off area for the water along this stretch of the EEH compared to Everard Nagar, within minutes, the waterlogging began to swell. Shailesh could feel it get worse and worse as he crawled through the water.

The rain lashed at the road like a tidal wave, its sweeping power so great it almost seemed to push his car backwards. Everywhere on the horizon was a sea of dark grey, an angry grey. With an intense cascade of white mist from the rain in the front. The rear-view mirror no longer offered any visibility either. There were other vehicles around, plenty of them, but in that moment, Shailesh felt very alone in a lop-sided battle against raging mother nature.

Mahesh got very, very agitated and pulled out his handkerchief to wipe off nervous drops of sweat from his face. He asked, "Will we make it?"

Shailesh didn't reply. He couldn't. His own heart was in his mouth too. He was praying desperately to make it so they could get through this, get on the

Amar Mahal flyover, hoping to find clear road on the other side.

As he approached the mouth of the flyover, the water was getting up to the car window. A minute's delay now could be costly, fatally so.

He pushed and pushed even as the engine started to sputter. He was concentrating so hard on keeping it moving he wasn't even keeping track of where they were.

And then, almost suddenly, he felt the car climb an elevation. He looked sideways and couldn't believe his eyes. They had started climbing the Amar Mahal flyover. They could breathe. They could live.

Without any conscious synchronisation, both Shailesh and Mahesh cried, "*Ganpati Bappa Morya!*"

Shailesh exhaled loudly.

Mahesh said, "My hands were trembling. My heart almost stopped beating."

Shailesh replied. "I had to tell mine not to stop. I needed to drive."

Mahesh hugged him tightly. Shailesh laughed and pleaded for him to release his grip so he could drive.

As Mahesh did so, he exclaimed, "Shailesh, you are my hero, my saviour."

"I still have some more saving to do, so hold it. And I am saving myself too."

Mahesh declared, "Now I am very confident you will do it. Man, how can I ever repay you?"

Shailesh winked and said, "*Goa mein yaad rakhna* (remember me when in Goa)."

4th September

Shailesh tossed and turned in bed.

He really wanted to sleep in a bit longer, but the bright light emanating from the morning sun appeared to implore him to arise.

Yesterday night, like most of the nights preceding the day of Ganesh Chaturthi, was a wash. As one '*sarvajanik mandal*' (public mandap) after the other welcomed their idol, the sound of loud music and firecrackers created a din that made it impossible to sleep until 12. Thereafter, sleep had eluded him for an hour more.

It was 7AM now but the sun shone bright, in stark contrast to yesterday's day of doom and gloom. He wanted some more sleep. His body still ached from yesterday's effort.

Just then, mother called out his name. In that loving and affectionate voice of hers that made it exceedingly difficult for him to get too pissed off at her for waking him up.

She added, "We need to do Ganesh Puja, ma. Are you getting up?"

He said, a bit cranky, "Yes, yes, I am."

She came over and stroked his hair gently. Embarrassed, he tried to brush her aside.

She said, "I know you must be very tired after yesterday. That's why I didn't disturb you until now. But I heard you moving about in bed."

"It's ok. I am awake. I wanted to sleep some more but the bloody sunshine won't let me to."

"Don't get angry at the sun, baba. It is helping me dry the clothes after yesterday's cloudburst."

Shailesh shrugged. He didn't want to argue the point. He got out of bed and headed to the bathroom.

As he sipped tea, he scrolled through Facebook on his phone.

One of the posts that caught his eye was from a group where people posted memories of Mumbai.

This post had the photo of the South Mumbai skyline (chockfull with towering highrises) with the person who made the post saying, "I left Mumbai in 1992 and have been living in New York for the last fifteen years. Looking at these photos, I feel like Mumbai is New York. But then, I remembered that New York is no match for Mumbai. East or West, Mumbai is the best."

Something about this post triggered Shailesh and he wrote an angry retort, "It is unfortunate that all these years of living in New York have neither cured your ignorance nor inane use of English. At least don't spread your ignorance to people who haven't seen New York."

As it happened, the commenter was online and replied immediately, "Dude, you don't even live in New York. You can't lecture me about ignorance."

Shailesh responded, "Exactly, I live in Mumbai, unlike you who left in 1992. And I have visited New York twice. So, unlike you, I know that New York is

New York and claiming that Mumbai is the best is just silly."

The commenter returned, "Ungrateful people like you don't deserve to be in Mumbai. You should be thrown out of Mumbai."

Shailesh wouldn't let go. He asked, "Again, you don't live here. What difference would it even make to you who does or doesn't live in Mumbai. When did you last visit Mumbai?"

The other shot back, "That's none of your business."

"So that means you have never visited Mumbai post-1992. Good."

"You're wrong. I have been here several times. And I have seen first hand how it has transformed. The airport is amazing, there are so many flyovers, the cars are so good, the malls are better than US."

"Have you tried looking out of the window from the flyovers? Because you didn't mention the slums at all."

"There is too much migration in Mumbai. The migrants should be kicked out."

"You should pray the US govt doesn't also think like you because then you know what will happen."

The other responded with choice insults and Shailesh in turn issued some of his own.

The ruckus had apparently attracted the attention of a moderator. Soon, Shailesh found the thread had disappeared. And when he tried to post comments on other posts in the group, he found the comment box would no longer appear. He had been banned from the group.

But the other guy hadn't been banned. Shailesh could see new comments from him on other posts.

Shailesh thought about taking it up with the moderator and asking why he had been banned and the other hadn't. But he soon decided against it. It just wasn't worth the time and effort.

And besides, most posts in the group were similarly over the top and jingoistic. Maybe that's why he had been banned and not the other guy. His 'negativity' was more offensive than the other's jingoism.

But his mood had been fouled by this discussion.

He had a scowl on his face as he munched through breakfast.

Mother noticed and asked sharply, "Did you have an argument with somebody online?"

He didn't reply.

She slapped her forehead. "You can't stay away from this even on the day of a festival?"

He sighed and said, "Well, the others keep writing nonsense, festival or no festival."

"Go on," She pressed. "Tell me what he said."

He related the whole exchange to her, leaving out the exact selection of unparliamentary words with which the two had addressed each other.

She said, "Ok, agreed that he was being ridiculous, but can't you just let people be?"

"I am not *not* letting him be by simply disagreeing with him."

"If you *only* disagreed with him, he wouldn't have been so confrontational with you either."

He sighed. He couldn't argue with that. He said, "It's just that it's so exasperating to read the same drivel again and again. And again."

"Good, so all the more reason you don't need to ruin your breakfast and tea by scrolling on the phone and getting into an argument."

He was irritated. "Ma, the phone isn't the problem."

"No," She pressed. "The arguing on it when you could enjoy breakfast is."

He scowled again.

She rubbed a hand through his hair and he shook his head like a dog protesting its master petting it once too often.

She said, "Go, have a bath and come. We need to start the puja before 9."

After *puja* and after helping himself to South Indian style *modaks* prepared lovingly by mother, he went back to bed for an afternoon siesta. The siesta turned out a bit longer than he had budgeted. He had fallen asleep at 1 and he woke up only at 5.

Almost as soon as he opened his eyes, rang out his mother's voice. "Shall I make tea for you ma?"

Startled, he asked, "How did you know I am awake?"

She smiled and said nothing, walking over to the kitchen instead.

As she made tea, she asked, "Shall we go over to see Ganpatis?"

"Now?" He asked wearily.

"Obviously not now! But the usual time, 7 ish."

"Hmmm…ok."

"What happened, da? Had you made plans with friends for the evening? I asked because you used to love seeing Ganesh *mandals* on Chaturthi."

True enough, he did used to.

He could still remember the first time he had seen a ten feet idol. His then barely four feet self had had his mind blown. Man, he had had to really crane his neck to get a good look at the idol's face.

He also remembered the first 'themed' *mandal* he had visited. It was based on a Vaishno Devi theme and the set consisted of a dark cave with barely visible stairs that the devotees were required to peruse of to get to the Ganesha idol. It was a different time, he thought, when such setups didn't lead to stampedes. And nor were people so cynical as to ask why they were required to subject themselves to so much effort and risk just to get a glimpse of a large Ganesha idol.

Could that innocence ever be recaptured? Perhaps not. Perhaps it was more an illusion than an existence of innocence. Perhaps there had been curmudgeonly uncles then too who had commented caustically on such Vaishno Devi-like experiments. And perhaps it had simply been he in his childhood innocence who had never paid heed to such quips. Or perhaps, there was more to it than that. Perhaps something had changed.

Well, one way to find out could be to just…revisit the experience all over again?

He said, "Ok, let's go."

Mother beamed brightly at this. How innocently joyful she still was, after all these years! He dreamed that one day he could be that way too. It certainly seemed to be a lighter existence. Maybe it also entailed not having people like Ajay sir in your life, though!

At 7, they headed out to a *mandal* right on LBS Road. It was of some shopkeepers' association that he could no longer recall the name of. But he knew where to find it each year. The locations had become fairly baked-in by now.

As they were about to get into the enclosed space, something about the arch welcoming devotees struck him.

The top of the arch had a 20 feet wide poster (roughly the width of the lane the *mandal* was on).

The most prominent image on the poster was… of the corporators co-sponsoring the *mandal*. With their names written in the boldest possible font as well.

Followed by the words, "*Hardik Abhinandan.*"

On the bottom right, in a pitiful corner, was an image of Lord Ganesha.

Yes, this was it.

Maybe he was remembering it all wrong but somehow, he didn't remember such posters adorning that Vaishno Devi themed *mandal* he had been to in his childhood.

He silently accompanied mother, not wishing to disturb the moment for her.

But once they were done offering prayers to the idol in that *mandal*, he said, "Let's go home."

"But dear, we only saw one mandal."

"One is too many. Let's go."

"What happened, ma?" Her concern was so heartfelt he almost didn't want to say what he was about to.

He said, "It seems that these *mandals* worship the corporators more than Ganesha Himself. And I came to worship Ganesha."

"Ganesha will take care of the corporators." She replied. "What is important is praying to Ganesha."

"And that we can do at home."

"But it's not the same as visiting a *mandal*."

"Yes, because at home, you wouldn't have to get past the photos of these corporators to get to Ganesha."

"Again, the point is simply about worshipping Ganesha. Forget about the corporators."

"But they want me to remember them. That's why their photos are bigger than that of Ganesha. It seems like Ganesha doesn't matter. Maybe He indeed doesn't. Maybe the ritual isn't *really* about worshipping Him."

She snapped, "When did you start becoming an atheist?"

He was confused. "Well, I don't *think* I am an atheist."

"Are you sure? Because you're complicating this way more than you need to."

"Maybe you're right. And maybe I just can't help complicate things."

She slapped her forehand vigorously.

He said, sadly, "I am sorry, ma. Come, let's go to some more mandals."

But she was way too upset by now. "There's no need. We'll just do *aarti* at home."

He trudged along. Well, this wasn't how he had imagined his holiday would pan out. Was he being unreasonable? He was damned if he could figure that one out.

He felt a bit guilty because as a kid, back when they had lived in a large multi-building 'colony' in Dombivli, mother had trained and pushed him to participate in their Housing Society organized Ganeshotsav celebrations. They would install a Ganesh idol in their Society compound and prayers would be held throughout the day. But, in the evenings, there would be programmes for adults and the kids. Typically, for the kids there would be quiz competitions, skits and music contests. He had sung a popular song from the Aamir Khan starrer *Hum Hain Raahi Pyar Ke* and won the 1st prize. How thrilling! Being called the next Kumar Sanu worked wonders for his ego.

Was he haunted by a past that could never return, because of how he remembered this past free of warts and as a beautiful dream, a dream that clashed with the nightmare he seemed to have to live day in and day out?

On a whim, he called a number where he thought he might get answers. Melvin Fernandes. He had known him in his Dombivli days. Melvin was ten years older but used to play cricket with little kids like Shailesh, slowing down his pace by a tenth (though the bounce, coming off his 5 10" height and a straight on action, was still way too much for Shailesh to deal with).

Melvin also used to listen to rock music and played guitar. He knew of only a few rock loving guys in Mumbai and nobody, nobody who hailed from Dombivli. He knew Melvin had kept in touch with his passion while working for an advertising agency by day. He also knew of Melvin as a patient and sympathetic listener. They had kept intermittently in touch through the years. And the conversations had grown progressively more serious as Shailesh had grown into his twenties.

Melvin picked up after a few rings.

"Dude! Happy Ganesh!" Melvin greeted him, boisterous and cheerful as always.

"Hi Melvin, thanks and wishing you the same. How're you? Long time."

"I am fine but it's always a long time between your calls." Melvin complained.

"It's also a long time between *your* calls." Shailesh pointed out.

"Good show, good show. So…what can I do for you?" Melvin intuited that this would be agony uncle time.

"Melvin, there used to be this rock show in South Mumbai, right?"

"Why? Do you wanna go?" Melvin teased him.

"No re. You know very well that rock music and me are poles apart. But I remember you mentioning about it."

"I-Rock. Used to be at Rang Bhawan. Stopped a long time ago. Some noise pollution rules. Imagine, in that area, right next to Xaviers."

"Right, now I remember."

"But why are you asking now, all of a sudden?"

"You have played there, right?"

"The year I was going to was the year the court order came. No."

"Where do you play these days?"

Melvin shrugged. "Just pubs here and there. Recently they started an Anti-Social in Lower Parel. You know, the one in Khar shut down."

"Would you have loved to play at Rang Bhawan?"

"Oh, for sure, dude. It sucks that way. The big artists come and play in front of huge crowds at BKC or DY Patil. But there's no place, other than these pubs, for us."

"Do you think Mumbai kinda sucks these days?"

"I haven't thought about it and I don't particularly want to."

"And that's because?"

"You know… I know you don't listen to rock music but there's a line from a song I love. It goes 'Do you want the truth or do you want your sanity?'.

I am fourth generation in this city, man. There's no way I can go anywhere else."

"But does it hurt that there's no place to show off your music?"

"I have never thought about it as showing off. I know that the long hair and stuff makes people think I am showing off but I have always only wanted to share my music. But I need someone to share to."

"There's nobody?"

"I wouldn't exactly say that. But if you put me back in 2003, when they shut down Rang Bhawan, and asked me what I thought the scene would look like in Mumbai after so many years, then I would have described a scenario that would look way optimistic compared to today."

"Hmmm….so in that respect, the city hasn't grown."

"Maybe. You know, I really don't know. Maybe I was just naïve then. I try not to think about it, because who knows if I am simply projecting an internal midlife crisis to make up a grand narrative.

And I don't know nearly enough about all that, so I am going to shut up."

"Interesting."

"Ok but why do you suddenly find all this interesting?"

Shailesh's reply was too enigmatic to satisfy Melvin. "I am thinking about things. And looking for answers."

5th September

Shailesh was in office by 9. Ajay wouldn't be in today. He had known this in advance; Ajay had scheduled leave on 5th and 6th and would return only on Monday the 9th.

No, Shailesh's reason for being in office early had nothing to do with Ajay, but an important conversation he needed to have before he got overwhelmed with emails, calls or colleagues requiring inputs on some or the other thing.

At 9.15, he called up Avesh. Avesh was the assistant of Hetal Padia, a property lawyer based out of Navi Mumbai. He had been prospecting a 3BHK home in Vashi. In fact, he had made an advance of 15 lakhs to the seller. This he had made basis Mrs Padia's assurance that the papers were in order.

However, it had been a month and a half and the CIDCO transfer was not coming through. He had wanted to move in (in a manner of speaking, as he didn't intend to shift right away) on Ganesh Chaturthi but now, even Anant Chaturdashi would not be possible.

Avesh picked up the call after several rings. Not a good sign, Shailesh thought.

"Hello sir." Avesh was ultra deferential.

"Hello, Mr Avesh. How are you?"

"I am fine sir. How are you?"

"I am fine. I would be better if you had some good news."

"Not yet, sir." Avesh laughed nervously.

"What is it, Mr Avesh? What is going on? Please don't hide anything anymore."

"Sir, sir, I am not hiding anything."

"Glad to hear that. In that case, tell me everything, all the problems with the property."

"Sir, there is absolutely nothing wrong with the property."

"Then why is the CIDCO transfer not getting approved?"

"Sir, the issue is of CIDCO itself."

"Meaning?"

"The plot on which the property stands is a bungalow plot."

"I am aware of that. And permission was granted to build a multi storey residential apartment building on it instead. Like so many other properties in the area."

"Sir, now CIDCO is saying that should not have been done."

"Ok, but they gave CIDCO transfer to the first seller and then to Sachin (the current seller) when he bought the property."

"They're saying just because they made a mistake then doesn't mean they need to repeat it now."

"What?"

"Sir, please don't get angry."

"I am not getting angry with you. Well, on second thoughts, I *am*. You should have advised me of this problem when I brought the papers to you."

"Normally, these things are easily managed sir."

"It's not about managing. It's about whether on the day, it's a clear-cut green signal or not. You didn't have that, am I right?"

"Sir…"

"Now what do we do?"

"Sir, there is no problem with the property. Even the CIDCO transfer issue will be eventually sorted out."

"*Eventually?*"

"Sir, it will take time."

"But I need CIDCO transfer to get a home loan."

"Sir, I can connect you to a co-operative bank."

"I want to do it the straightforward way, Mr Avesh."

"Sir, that is a bit difficult now."

Shailesh was furious but he also appreciated the futility of upbraiding Avesh any further about this. The deed was done. He needed to speak to Sachin to sort this out.

He called up Sachin.

"Yes, Shailesh?" Sachin answered the phone.

"Hi Sachin."

"Hi, tell me."

"We have a problem. The CIDCO transfer is not coming through."

"There is no problem with the title for this property. We have conveyance."

"But I need a loan and the bank is not ready to give me a loan without CIDCO transfer."

"Look, I had told you to go to Mr Jaiswal as he had done the papers for me. And you insisted on going to Mrs Padia."

"Sachin, I really like this property and if I could buy it without a loan, I would."

"But you cannot. So what do we do now?"

"I need to call it off, Sachin. I am sorry."

"Fair enough, but I already gave your advance to the bank to release the papers."

"How much can you give me back?"

"You do understand that I don't *have* to give you back anything?"

Shailesh was silent. He had hoped Sachin wouldn't go there.

After a minute of silence, Sachin said, "Within one month, I can pay you back 5 lakhs. The remaining 10 lakhs will take time. I don't have that kind of money. If I did, I would have paid off the loan myself."

Shailesh was sure Sachin *did* have the entire 15 lakhs in bank as of right now. But there was nothing he could do.

He pleaded. "Can you at least pay off 10 lakhs in three months? And the last 5, you may take your time."

Sachin was non-committal. "I will try. I cannot promise. You understand, this is effectively a loss for me."

"I understand. I do."

"I did not even take a token from you when I handed over the photocopy of the papers. If your lawyer is incompetent, that's not my fault."

"No, it isn't. I do understand."

"Look, I will definitely pay you back the 15 lakhs. It *is* your money, not mine. But I cannot do so right way."

"Fair enough, Sachin."

They exchanged pleasantries and disconnected the call.

He immediately called up mother.

From his tone of greeting, she sensed something amiss and asked, "Anything wrong, ma?"

"Anything? Everything went wrong."

"Calm down, calm down. Wherever you are, just sit down and have a glass of water first."

Across the phone, she persuaded him to gratefully obey and listened as she heard him gulp down the water.

"OK, now tell me, what's wrong?"

"It's the house."

"Hmmm."

"Well, we won't be able to buy it."

Mother was aghast. "But why?"

"I spoke to Avesh. He has no degree of confidence that he will get the CIDCO transfer."

"But when we showed the papers to Hetal madam, they said everything's fine."

"That's what I told him. He has no answer. How does it matter to him anyway? They collect their fees in advance. Maybe this is the reason why."

"What's Sachin saying?"

"He said he can't return such a big amount in one go."

"So?"

"He will pay 5 lakhs within a month."

"The remaining?"

"There's no timetable for that."

"Is it gone?"

"*Maybe* not. But I will have to do without it for a long time."

"Not I, we. We're all in it together."

"Well, are we?"

"Shailesh?"

"I was the one out of the three who said we shouldn't go for this. And the loan has to come in my name. You two overruled me."

"We didn't overrule you, pa. We just disagreed. And you gave in."

"That's a nice way to put it."

"Shailesh, stop it! This blame game won't get us anywhere. Anyway, why don't I ask Murugan? He may know fixers in Navi Mumbai who can get the CIDCO transfer."

"Suppose he helps us get it and one day I need to sell the flat and the fixer is no more? How will my buyer get the CIDCO transfer?"

"Come on, surely they will fix the issue by then."

"You're more optimistic than I am."

"Take a chance, pa."

"It's my money and it's gone down the drain. I won't."

"We will give you a loan. Don't worry about the money."

"No need. Let's not compound the mistake. My idea is we will cut the losses right here and escape."

"But we need a new flat."

"We don't, not really. There's just the three of us."

"And when you marry?"

"We'll cross that bridge when we get there."

Just then, he noticed that there was another call on whatsapp and told mother he would call her back.

It was the HR manager from the company offering the Zimbabwean opportunity.

She said, "Hi Shailesh. We are scheduling you for Saturday 2.30 PM. Pl make yourself available."

"Sure."

"I am also sending an email, so please reply with your confirmation."

"Ok."

With that, she hung up.

He called mother back and said, "The Zimbabwe people. They are interviewing me on Saturday."

She beamed. "Very good. Do well. All the best, da."

"Thanks ma, but I really need to think about it. Do you think I should talk to Pa?"

"He is back on Sunday anyway. You go through with the interview first."

"What if they make an offer?"

"We'll cross that bridge when we get there."

She had a big smile on her face as she said that. He could see the smile on the other end of the line and couldn't help smiling back.

***

It was a relatively slow day at work without Ajay sir to invent something or the other to keep them all glued to their laptop screens.

He came back at 11.30 for a second tea, which he usually avoided.

He sat down and watched the cup, as his mind drifted elsewhere.

"Lost in thought, Shailesh?" The question gave him a start as his attention was returned to the present. It was Mansi.

"Yes, sorry ma'am."

Mansi madam. A tallish, dusky woman in her forties who somehow still looked as if she was in her late 20s. Fit, athletic even (she played tennis daily and on occasion handed out humiliating bagels to crushed masculine egos) and ever-smiling. A ray or rather a blast of sunshine in the overcast pall of gloom that was his org.

He started to drink the tea very quickly and she laughed as she sat on the chair opposite his.

"It's fine. It's ok to chill out one day." She said and winked.

He smiled and said, "Thank you ma'am."

She asked, "So…what's making a young man like you so pensive?"

She wasn't exactly old herself but Shailesh decided against contesting that point.

Instead, he said, "Lots of stuff."

And then, he found himself dropping his guard and briefly reciting the events of the last couple of days. The drive through hellish rains, the bitter Ganesh Puja experience and now this latest setback.

She shook her head and said, "Don't think so much. You're an accountant, not a philosopher."

"So…you don't discount the validity of what I have observed."

"Maybe not. But there is always something going on in most people's lives. Whatcha gonna do? Just gotta get on with it."

Her eyes lit up as something came to mind. "Oh, I once dated this guy who listened to weird music. And one line he used to quote from a song he loved somehow struck me as not weird at all and in fact quite profound. It was, 'Do you want the truth? Or do you want your sanity?' He would keep quoting that line. Think about that, Shailesh. Fine, you have hit the nail on the head when it comes to the reality of living in Mumbai. But is that going to help you change that reality?"

"I guess not."

"By the way," She was on a tangent now. "Speaking of dating, don't you have any girls in your life? That will banish these feelings."

He sighed heavily. "Had one about a couple of years back."

"Had?"

"Yeah…we broke up."

"And you don't want to experience heartbreak again."

"I would like to experience love again. But maybe after a while, after the heartbreak no longer stings."

"Hmmm. Anyway, I hope you got the hint. Take your mind away from these thoughts. Demons be that way. I would offer you a position in my team but nobody's leaving now."

"Why would they?" He said to himself. With a manager like her, he too would probably be happier than he was now.

As he got up, he noticed someone conspicuous by their unexpected absence today. As he walked back to his desk, he asked Kunal, "Where's Hasmukh?"

Hasmukh was the moniker the folks in the office had given to Harshal, the perma-temp. He had been here since the day this office had been built and he was still here ten years later. And he was still a temp, on the rolls of a third-party agency rather than the organization. He had a permanent smile affixed on his face. That was the best option he had to deal with the hand dealt him by fate.

Kunal said gloomily, "Down with dengue, yaar."

"What happened?"

"The trains weren't running by the time he was able to leave. So he had to wade through waterlogged roads to get home. Fell sick the same night."

Shailesh mouthed a "Damn!" and shook his head and he got back to work.

He trudged through the rest of the day.

At 5 PM, he looked at his watch and then at Kunal who made a quizzical gesture. He gestured to get going. Kunal pointed to his laptop with a frown.

Shailesh understood. Kunal was never super eager to leave work. Shailesh supposed going home to a much more cramped living space in South Mumbai was less attractive. Still…if he lived *that* close to Marine Drive, he would go there every day….

Ah, he had an idea. If he left right away, he could get there before sunset. There was time. It was a clear day too. And he hoped it would flush out the negativity around the failed home deal from his system.

And so, as he hopped onto the elevator, he put in a request on the aggregators for a cab ride to Marine Drive. He gave NCPA as the landmark…you couldn't very well say 'Marine Drive' on Ola!

By some good fortune, a cab was available and just a minute away. In fact, as he got out of the office block, a spanking new Dzire Tour lay in wait for him. He hopped on merrily.

There wasn't much traffic, being that he was heading down South precisely when people would be beginning the long and painful trek up North to get home.

In ten minutes, they were ascending the Bandra Worli Sealink. The driver excitedly informed him that once the Coastal Road was inaugurated, he would be able to speed across from Bandra to Princess Street Flyover.

True, thought Shailesh, but he wondered too. He remembered when there had been no flyover over Maheshwari Udyan (or King's Circle as the old timers called it). He knew there hadn't been over the head of Khodadad Circle either. If you went far back enough in time, there used to be a roundabout at Heera Panna junction too. The view along the Haji Ali seaface had already changed beyond recognition and the Coastal Road was yet to be inaugurated.

This was supposed to the linear march of progress but were they all simply going round and round the island with ever increasing intensity but with no destination in sight?

Lost as he was in his thoughts, he didn't realize that he was just ten minutes away from Marine Drive.

As they reached Ambassador Hotel, he asked the cabbie to take a U turn right there to stop along the promenade and end the ride. The cabbie protested that the destination was NCPA. Shailesh said he would be paying him the original fare anyway at which he readily acquiesced.

He got down and started walking along to NCPA.

It was always a beautiful day when it was evening at Marine Drive. He would never stop loving every moment he spent there. He couldn't explain it. It was a feeling he knew many other Mumbaiites shared and most likely, they too wouldn't be able to explain it. It was the place itself, yes, but also the memories it held for so many of the city's denizens.

He had been here on at least four separate occasions with his college friends. Sumedh, Vineet, Pradeep and Ashutosh. They were not only collegemates but classmates. They had all had other friends too in college but somehow, this band of five had stuck together tighter and cohered into a clique.

He remembered the time when Vineet, the fitness freak of the group, had suggested they walk from Chowpatty to Nariman Point. Ashutosh had protested but been dragged kicking and screaming the whole way anyway. Vineet never failed to remind Ashutosh of this incident whenever they meet.

Golly, it had been a long time since they had met. The last time had been just before the pandemic and that one had happened a year after the previous. They had vowed to keep in touch after getting out of college but it was a promise that had become harder and harder to keep. They did keep in touch, still, in a manner of speaking – on a whatsapp group called 'College Masti'.

He also had a very specific and vivid memory associated with Marine Drive and NCPA. Quite a few years back, he, who didn't know the first thing about Western classical music, had gone on a lark to attend a performance of Beethoven's Ninth Symphony at the NCPA and enjoyed it so much that he had walked out onto Marine Drive and taken in the breeze for a few minutes.

He looked to his left and there he was, right across the road from NCPA. He hadn't even noticed! Maybe it was because there was hardly any breeze. Here he was, standing right by the sea, with only the promenade wall and the tetrapods in the way. And yet, Marine Drive, even at nearly 6 PM felt just as hot as anywhere else in the city.

He looked wistfully out to the horizon and then, he saw what he had come all the way for. The sight of the sun gently setting. A sight that brought forth another visual from the memory bank.

He had come here more times than he could remember back in his articleship days when visiting the offices of an audit client in Nariman Point.

There had been days when he had come to their office from his firm's office in Dadar and taken the train to Churchgate to do so. Knowing that he needed to get there ASAP, he had still eschewed the long queues for bus or shared taxi rides to Nariman Point from Churchgate or even the shortcut via Eros. He had instead gone past Ambassador Hotel and turned left to walk on to Nariman Point…via Marine Drive.

There had been days during the audit when he had not been in the best of moods. And he had wandered down to Marine Drive on the pretext of fetching something to eat from the sandwich stalls in Nariman Point. Sitting there silently for ten to fifteen minutes, staring at the sea, at the horizon of blue nothingness, had made him at least momentarily forget whatever had got him down.

But he had never been able to see the sun setting on the Arabian Sea at Marine Drive. And he would today.

He watched silently for the next fifteen minutes as the sun approached closer and closer to the frontier of the sea on the horizon. The sight of the sun seemingly melting away into the water, illusory as it was, could only be savoured here at Marine Drive.

Which is why so many people gathered here. And the place was getting crowded now.

It was time to move on. Time seemed to stand still at Marine Drive. Or at....

Yes, he thought. He would go there too.

He hailed another cab for a ride to the other end of the Southern tip of the city.

Twenty minutes later, he got down at Apollo Bunder and beheld the majestic monument that is the Gateway of India.

In a city where almost every landmark of note had been renamed, nobody had bothered with the idea of renaming Gateway of India. It was in some ways unaccountable, this strange love Mumbaiites had for the city's British legacy. The fact that they had left behind these lovely buildings as well as laid the foundations for the railway network that had become the city's lifeline surely didn't excuse all the looting they had gleefully carried out. And yet, nothing matched the affection he, like so many other of his fellow Mumbaiites, had for the city's British era relics.

Perhaps, like Marine Drive, the timelessness of Gateway served as an anchor. As something to hold onto for those who had spent a long time, maybe too long of a time, in the city. As everything around you changed, you could still stand right next to Gateway and turn the pages of the photo album in your mind as the memories came flooding back.

He remembered the time he had gone along with his grandfather on a trip around South Mumbai. The trip had encompassed every corner of South Mumbai, from Nariman Point to Cuffe Parade to Gateway and everything en route. It was his grandfather who had told him that the specific style of architecture seen on the buildings along Marine Drive was called Art Deco. While the CSMT building was apparently in Italian Gothic style.

It had only been a couple of years since grandfather had passed away. The memories came flooding back indeed and so did the tears.

As he stood there silently, tears streaming down his eyes, the phone rang.

Mother asked, "Have you started, dear?"

He shook his head and said, "I am at Gateway."

She was astonished. "What are you doing there? Did you have some meeting with bankers?"

"No, I just…never mind. I am starting back for home now."

6th September

Shailesh was driving on the EEH when the rain came on heavily. It was the angry, tsunami-like downpour again. Fresh from his recent experience, he felt more than ready to take it on. He tightened the grip on the steering and sat up in a more upright posture to signal to the rain clouds that he was going to beat the daylights out of them this time.

As he did so, suddenly and without explanation, the roof of the car flew out. Suddenly, he found himself getting soaked in the rain. It was so intense the impact on his skin stung. How was this possible? How could the car's roof fly out? Make any of this make sense, he demanded.

He came to with a start. He found himself lying in bed, not driving a Nexon with its roof magically levitating in the rain. And the water was seepage from the ceiling. It was not a downpour and it didn't hurt but it was also right over his head.

He got out of bed angrily.

He called out to mother. The tone of his voice signalled to her that she'd better make it soon, before he exploded.

She had one look at the bedroom and she knew.

She said to him, "I will call Ravi."

"Didn't he say he was too big for this stuff last time?"

"Let's try. We don't have a lot of options if he doesn't want to take it up, you know."

Shailesh shook his head.

He helped move the cot away a little from the line of fire of the seepage spot. Then, he completed his morning routine of getting ready for work and carried on.

At about 10.30, his mother called Ravi.

"Hello madam."

"Hello Mr Ravi."

"Tell me madam."

"We have really bad seepage in our bedroom."

"So what should I do?"

She was more than a little taken aback by the tone.

"Well," She managed to say, "Could you come and repair it?"

"Madam, I don't take up these small jobs anymore. I told you before itself, madam."

"But I heard you had done plastering and toilet work for Mrs Desai." Mrs Desai was their neighbour.

"Madam, that was one time, because she kept requesting again and again. I won't do it again."

"But you finished the work at her home only 10 days back."

"Madam, I told you, no?"

"Ok, can you recommend someone else? This work is so urgent. Shailesh got woken up from his sleep because of the seepage. He is afraid to use that room now. And when uncle returns tomorrow, he will have to sleep on the sofa."

"Ok, ok, madam, I am coming, but this is last time."

So said he but the clock struck 12, then 3 and there was yet no sign of him.

She called him up again.

As soon as he picked up, she was on the offensive. "Ravi, you said you will come. Where are you?"

"Madam, I am in Andheri." He said, in a manner that suggested she ought to have already known this ostensibly obvious fact.

"Andheri!" She exclaimed, realizing he wouldn't be here for the next hour, maybe two hours even if he started right away.

"Yes, madam. I told you I am doing big contracts."

"But you said you will come."

"I am not denying that. I am still saying I will come."

"When?"

"Madam, my work at Andheri gets over at 7. After that, I will start from there."

"But by then…"

"Madam, I have to finish my work before I can come here. If it doesn't suit you, find someone else."

She sighed heavily. "Alright, you come. We will wait."

Shailesh left work at 5.30 again, taking advantage of the absence of Ajay sir.

As he walked out on to the road and towards his stop, he saw a sight that looked vaguely familiar.

Yeah, he was sure he didn't know too many middle aged men who rode Ducatis in Mumbai.

Just then, he spied the glitter of a toothy grin from within the helmet of the rider, who now waved at him.

The bike drew to a halt next to Shailesh, as Jahangir Screwvala alighted and, without hesitation, gave him a warm hug. He was wearing sunglasses and a bright yellow T-shirt paired with denims.

"*Kem cho?*" He asked (How are you in Gujarati).

"*Majama*, sir." Shailesh replied (I am fine, also in Gujarati).

"So, Sheru has grown up." Jahangir used to refer to him as Sheru.

"Yes, sir. I work in this building." Shailesh pointed to the office block.

"Come with me, let me treat you to some ice cream."

"Sir…" Shailesh protested feebly, knowing it would be in vain.

"Arre, come na? We have met after such a long time. Not far, I will take you to this place in Hill Road."

"In this traffic…"

"When has traffic ever been a problem for me?" Jahangir quipped, with a twinkle in his eye.

Shailesh smiled with trepidation.

The next 20 minutes were a blur. Shailesh closed his eyes. He knew if he dared open them, he would fall off the bike out of sheer fright at what was unfolding. Jahangir found gaps in Mumbai traffic that even the late Ayrton Senna would have baulked at as he zoomed and vroomed through gridlock.

Jahangir had clearly known this all the time, for, upon arriving at the ice cream parlour, he said, "Ok, now you can open your eyes."

Shailesh looked straight ahead. The display board of the shop was badly faded and he couldn't even make out the name.

Again, reading his mind, Jahangir said, "Don't worry about the name. This is the best butterscotch you will ever have. Trust me."

"I trusted your cost accounting lessons, sir. Of course I will trust you on this." Shailesh said.

Jahangir beamed.

He asked how things were going for Shailesh and Shailesh briefly recounted his experience thus far of working for Ajay sir.

Jahangir encouraged him, "You will always come across bosses like Ajay. Don't worry about it. There will be good bosses too."

"How about you, sir? I am sure you are still teaching."

"Yes, but under my own roof."

Shailesh whistled.

Jahangir nodded. "Yes. I no longer teach for other classes. Only my own. And the rest of my time goes in running the business. I have two branches, one in Ghatkopar and another in Bandra. I was on my way to the Bandra branch and that's how I saw you today."

"So you must have made a lot of money just teaching." Shailesh wondered.

Jahangir shook his head. "Nothing like that. I was able to influence a friend in a bank to give a loan. I took a big loan. I had to mortgage my home for it. But it was worth it."

"But if it had failed…"

"I would have gone back to teaching. And yes, I would have lost the home. I would have had to stay on rent. No problem, *kar lete* (I'd have done it)."

Jahangir continued. "See, you know how my methods of teaching were. I am regarded as unorthodox because I try to find the most interesting way to teach the concepts to the students. I will tell you stories about cricket, politics, film industry and you will all keep laughing but I know you will still remember something essential about the concepts at the end of the lesson.

"The proprietor of SN Classes also understood this because he was a teacher himself. Then, he had a massive heart attack and died. His son took over and he had no clue. Some intolerant students complained and the son asked me to change my style. That's when I knew I had to find a way to do it my way. Not because of ego, but because I do believe in the way I teach, that the students benefit from it. I believe this because of the calls I get from them thanking me for the lectures. And it is those messages that mean everything to me. If I can help you on your journey in any way, that means more than anything else to me."

"More than a Ducati?" Shailesh joked.

"I got the Ducati because the BMW had become too old."

"Oh!"

"Yes, back to pavilion for the BMW. Now a new bat to do the batting and hit the traffic for a six."

"By the way, sir, I meant to ask, you look so fit now. You have lost weight. Have you started playing?"

Jahangir smiled. "Yes, but not cricket."

"Then?"

"I am playing tennis. I play senior age group tournaments. I have even won prize money."

Shailesh laughed. "Not as if you need the money."

"*Yaar*, if I only did what I need to do for money, I wouldn't be able to live. Do you know that I organize South Mumbai heritage tours every Sunday morning? Absolutely free. I spend money out of my pocket to get there and circulate booklets to the tourists. I keep the groups limited to twenty but I don't do it for money."

"But what do you get out of it?"

Jahangir shrugged. "Sheru, if I tried to define it like that, I would stop doing all those things. I get so much joy from sharing my passion for…so many things. I also give lec-dems on motorcycles. There are other enthusiasts in the city and they have come to know about me. They want to get some benefit out of my knowledge, so why not?

"As it is, because of me, Parsi population in Mumbai is going to go down. I never married. I don't have children. At least I can give something back to the city while I am alive."

"But why would you give back to this city which takes so much from you?"

Jahangir smiled. "I don't look at it that way. It is not a transaction. I have not lived in any city other than Mumbai since birth. Now that I can give back something, I would like to."

He continued, "By the way, my friend has an art exhibition on Sunday. You are most welcome to attend."

Shailesh made a face.

Jahangir sighed a little and said, "Look, I know that experience really discouraged you. But getting negative won't help, no?"

Jahangir was referring to the time when Shailesh had written an article about a famous composer and forwarded it to his son, only for his effort to be met with indifference.

Shailesh shrugged, "That experience taught me that this is not a city of dreams. Rather, this is the city where dreams die. Except one dream. There is only one dream everybody seems to have in Mumbai — to make more and more money. And it's never enough."

"I am not after more and more money, no?" Jahangir pointed out.

Shailesh got up. He had finished the ice cream and it was also getting to 6.30 now.

He said, "Sir, you have been and always will be an inspiration. But maybe I need more time to get to where I can make something out of that inspiration."

Jahangir nodded and said, "Take your time. But not too much time. If you want to do something, do it now. Do it when you're wrong. Remember that song, no? *Jawaani phir na aaye!*"

As Jahangir, never the best dancer, comically moved his hips as he sang well out of tune, Shailesh laughed and shook his head.

It had been fun, it had given him food for thought too, but he really did need to go.

As they parted ways, Jahangir asked again, "You will come for the exhibition, no?"

Shailesh groaned. "I will try, sir. But Sundays, I need to rest. Going all the way to South Mumbai on a Sunday…"

His voice trailed.

Jahangir nodded in understanding. But the twinkle in his eyes had been replaced by a tinge of sadness.

It was 8.15 by the time Shailesh got home.

He found the bedroom door tightly shut.

As he was about to open the door, mother rushed screaming and stood as a bodyguard between him and the door as he was about to burn it.

Amused and irritated, he asked, "Will you let me open it please?"

"If you want the entire house to be flooded." She retorted.

"What? I don't understand."

"The seepage." She reminded him.

"Seepage?" He was baffled. "But I thought you had called Ravi?"

"I did. But he hasn't come yet."

"What!"

She nodded. "He must be on his way now. Was wrapping up a job at Andheri."

"What time did he say he was leaving from there?"

"Around 7."

"But in that case, he won't be here before 9."

She shrugged helplessly.

"But that's a disaster, ma." Shailesh was very upset and angry.

"Well, tell me you know of any other mason and I will call him next time."

Shailesh felt defensive. "I am not blaming you. It's just…"

"It is what it is. So let's grit our teeth till he comes. There's nothing else we can do."

"Well, we could eat. I am hungry." He quipped.

She smiled and went into the kitchen to conjure up some magic dosas to placate her son.

Over the next twenty minutes or so, they munched their dinner in silence with an RD Burman jukebox playing on Shailesh's phone.

As they finished and put their plates away, the doorbell rang. And within seconds, a second time. And a third time. Whoever was perusing of the doorbell was either an impatient sort or was just super angry. Shailesh hoped for the former.

He opened and found himself staring at Amit Banerjee, their neighbour who lived in the flat immediately downstairs. He gulped. He knew what was coming.

He greeted him warmly. "Hello uncle."

Mr Banerjee nodded as if he wished to acknowledge the greeting while simultaneously also moving onto the business at hand ASAP.

Mr Banerjee spoke up. "There is a lot of leakage from your bedroom. It's seeping into ours now."

Mother gatecrashed into the conversation. "Hello, Mr Banerjee. Yes, yes, there is seepage in our ceiling and we are waiting for the mason to come."

"But madam, I cannot wait. If there is seepage in my ceiling, it means it's serious. Can I see your bedroom?"

"I wouldn't advise it."

"So the seepage is that bad."

She persisted. "He should be here any minute."

"But he won't be here with a magic wand, madam. He will take time to repair it."

"Mr Banerjee, I have been following up with the mason since morning."

"Then get another mason. Who is your mason?"

"Ravi."

Mr Banerjee shrugged. That was his man too.

"We should find another mason. This guy is no good." He barked.

"I am asking again, do you know of another mason?"

"Madam, you can't blame it on the mason and escape. The problem is not getting solved."

She was exasperated now. "Sir, I don't know how to repair this and neither does my son. If you know someone who can or if you can repair it yourself, you are most welcome to."

"What!" Mr Banerjee was incensed. "First you harass me by spoiling my house and then you ask me to fix it myself."

"You make it sound like I did it intentionally."

"From your attitude, it sounds like you did."

"As if your attitude has been super reasonable." Shailesh could no longer restrain himself. "Just because the name of the building is Sapna Kunj, everyone seems to think the building maintenance can be done in dreams instead of reality."

Mr Banerjee fumed. "Like mother, like son. Enough! I will complain to the secretary."

"Please do," Shailesh added fuel to the fire. "If the secretary didn't use up all the water in the Thane Creek to clean his flat, we wouldn't have had seepage in the first place."

Mr Banerjee was adamant, "Doesn't matter. Doesn't make it acceptable for you to trouble me. I will still complain."

Just at this moment, the doorbell rang.

Mother opened the door.

It was Ravi. He asked, "Madam, please show me where the leak is."

"About time, huh!" Shailesh whistled.

Mr Banerjee continued fuming, "This is no good. He has come just now. He will take a lot of time to finish. Then he will say it can't be repaired today and he needs to come back tomorrow. Until then, am I supposed to get drenched even when I am not outdoors?"

Mother acted with lightning speed and, with the flair of a magician pulling a rabbit out of the hat, revealed a box of sweets that had been lying well-concealed in the fridge.

She offered it to Mr Banerjee.

He scowled. "What is this? Do you think I am a school child to give me candies to stop crying?"

She replied without hesitation. "*Sandesh*. Got it from Sweet Bengal."

He couldn't conceal a big smile on his face but nevertheless tried to sound dismissive. "I have had it hundreds of times in Kolkata."

"Sir, I will need a day to get *Sandesh* from Kolkata for you. But you can have this right now."

"Don't bribe me."

"I am not. I am treating you. I am thanking you for being an understanding, considerate and co-operative neighbour."

"I have no intention of being one." He protested but the volume of his voice had dropped. He was grinning ear to ear now.

Shailesh stepped back in. "Uncle, I will get on Ravi's case and see to it he repairs this right now. And I will also ask him to go down and visit your house immediately after finishing ours."

"Ok, ok," Mr Banerjee said, feeling more and more pressure to acquiesce.

He kept looking lovingly at the box of *Sandesh* as he walked out of their flat.

When he was gone, mother and Shailesh took one look at each other and started laughing at one and the same time.

Once they were done hurting their bellies, Shailesh asked, "Ma, where did you get that *Sandesh* from?"

"Monica aunty came today. Remember her?"

He did. She had been a neighbour during their days of living in Dombivli. She had upgraded herself much more significantly…and now lived in Santa Cruz.

Mother continued, "She gave us these sweets. I had meant to offer them to you along with the dosas but forgot about it. Sorry."

He shook his head. "No, it's good you didn't. It was our trump card today. It saved us from the wrath of the Bengal Tiger."

At this, they shared another bout of laughter.

7th September

The sunlight was creeping in. Drat! Today of all days, the rain just *had* to stop, huh. On a weekend when he wanted to tuck in for some more time. He pulled the blanket over his head, refusing to yield.

And just then, he heard his mother calling out his name. He tucked in deeper into the blanket, pretending to be too soundly asleep to hear her.

This, however, only made her intensify her efforts! She kept calling out to him. She entered the bedroom and continued calling out his name.

When she got right by the bedside, he finally pulled down the blanket in exasperation and asked, "What is it, ma?"

"It's 8, da. Get up."

"What for? It's Saturday."

"You have an interview."

"Ma, it's at 2.30."

"They could always reschedule. Prepare early and be ready so that you can give your best shot."

"Anyway, the deed is done. I won't get sleep now. Might as well get up."

As he lazily munched on corn flakes, the phone rang.

It was the HR manager. What now, were they cancelling?

He took the call and said, "Hi?"

"Hi, Shailesh. Sorry to ask at such short notice but are you free to attend the interview at 12.30?"

Wow, mother had some serious intuition, huh!

He had half a mind to say he wasn't free. But he had already gotten up. Maybe with the interview out of the way, he would have more of the rest of the day to look forward to.

He said, "Yes, I am free. I will be able to attend at 12.30."

"Great! So I will send you a revised meeting link shortly on email."

He put on a full arm shirt for the first time in a very long time on a Saturday. He wondered what that said about what a stint in Zimbabwe would look like. He told himself he would cross that bridge when he got there.

He logged into the Zoom link at 12:25.

The clock struck 12:30.

Five more minutes passed. And then another five.

He recalled the time a recruiter had requested for a Sunday 9AM interview even after he had told him he needed to leave home at 10 to catch a flight and then didn't appear on the call up to 9.10, which was when Shailesh had logged off in disgust and thereafter refused to take any of the recruiter's calls.

He thought about whether he should repeat that stunt when he saw the link stirring to life at last. He had been 'accepted'.

Two people were in the call. One was the HR manager who had been speaking to him.

The other was, presumably, his reporting manager. Yes, the name said Mukesh Sarda. He had seen his name on the invite. Mukesh had a stern expression and Shailesh sussed out an upright posture even from what he could see of him on video.

Presently, the HR manager made the introductions and opened the floor to Mukesh.

He smiled warmly for the first time.

He said, "Good afternoon, Shailesh. It is still morning here in Zimbabwe. How are you?"

"I am fine sir."

Mukesh did *not* tell him not to use sir. Shailesh made a mental note of that.

Mukesh said, "Sorry for rescheduling this interview at the last minute. Only yesterday evening, Head Office scheduled a call from 10.30 to 12.30 today so the original schedule was not possible anymore. It was too late by then to inform you, so we had to let you know today."

"It is ok sir. I don't have office today."

"OK but here you will have office on Saturdays. It will be a half day, but you will be required in office. You need to be comfortable with that."

Shailesh had given that a thought. He wasn't super chuffed about having to work on Saturdays, but he knew that if he indicated any reluctance or dissatisfaction, he wouldn't be shortlisted. While he wasn't sure he wanted this assignment, he did want to put his best foot forward in the interview.

Accordingly, he said, "Sir, it is not a problem."

With that, Mukesh moved to the usual interview territory of questions about Shailesh's background, his current job and his technical skills.

Mukesh then came to the question of relocating to Zimbabwe.

"I hope you are aware of the benefits and facilities provided by the company for this role, but I will reconfirm for you. You will get accommodation and along with, your electricity and cooking gas expense will be reimbursed. Internet facility will also be provided in the accommodation. The company will provide vehicle for pickup and drop. I will send you photos of my accommodation and the locality. But understand that, as per your salary structure, you may not necessarily be able to afford the same standard of accommodation. Now you can ask us any questions you have regarding this assignment."

"Sir, how is water and petrol availability? I have come across worrying reports on the net."

Mukesh smiled. "The first lesson for you to learn when you decide to work in Africa is to ignore the media. They present a picture that is very different from the reality. The reality is Zimbabwe had issues with fuel availability many years back but as of now, there is nothing. I have been working here for two years and haven't faced any problems at all.

"Now coming to water supply, once in a while, you might have issues but again, it will not be something unmanageable. Definitely don't expect everything to be like India. In India, you will not find so less pollution, so little traffic in any big city. So, you have to take the good and the bad as a package."

"Sir, I was going to ask about that. What will be the travel time to office typically?"

"Unless you specifically want to go and stay somewhere far away, not more than twenty minutes. Don't even worry about it."

"And will I be able to drive in Zimbabwe? I mean, is it safe?"

"Very safe. Nothing to worry."

Mukesh noticed the doubtful expression on Shailesh's face and added, "Look, you might think I am just marketing this country so that you accept to work here. But let me tell you that I had also never worked in Zimbabwe or anywhere else in Africa before I took up this assignment. My previous assignment was in Bengaluru. If there was something horribly wrong here, I would have gone back without wasting any time. Rest assured that Zimbabwe is safe. The only thing you need to have to be able to drive here is a driving licence. So I hope you have one."

"I do, sir."

"Good. We will talk in more detail if you are selected and if you accept the offer. But what I want to tell you is don't be afraid, don't be anxious. But also keep an open mind. Don't expect everything to be like India. This is not India, this is Zimbabwe."

"I would like to know what that means."

Mukesh laughed. "You will come to know. We don't spoil the experience for anyone."

With that, he and the HR manager concluded the interview.

As Shailesh got up from the chair to stretch his legs, mother rushed into the room.

"Yes, how did it go?"

Shailesh shrugged. "It went very well."

"Do you think they will select you?"

"I can't say for sure but…maybe. I would even say it looks likely."

She clapped enthusiastically. "Wonderful! I and pa will come and see you there. We will have to buy woollens. Kittu Mama said it gets very cold there in winter."

Shailesh shook his head in amusement. "Let's wait and see. I haven't made up my mind yet. I need to…"

His thoughts were interrupted by the sound of a whatsapp notification.

He checked the phone. He had received some messages from Mukesh.

As Mukesh had said he would, he had shared some photos.

There were a few photos of what was ostensibly his accommodation in Zimbabwe.

It appeared to be a standalone home and seemed to have three bedrooms. The living room and dining space was very spacious and the whole décor was very elegant and classy. It looked very…British.

The home also appeared to have a front yard and a back yard. The lawns on both were immaculately maintained.

There were also a few photos of the locality. It appeared to be a residential locality, looking leafy and quiet like a tony residential area in Mumbai.

But instead of high rises, all he could see were standalone homes with the odd G+3 low-rise. Also noticeable was the landscaping along the kerbs. It was beautiful. In fact, there seemed to be ample space for the kerbs so that even with the road only being two lanes wide, it didn't seem to be sandwiched by the homes in the way it would be in Mumbai.

Mother had been looking at the photos all the while too.

She beamed excitedly. "Did you see those photos? So nice, na?"

"Ma, he's the CFO. Obviously, he will have a very good accommodation."

"Yes, yes, but tell me, does your Ajay sir have such a nice house either?"

"No but that's because he's more miserly than Uncle Scrooge."

"But even if he wasn't, where in Mumbai do you think you will find such a home?"

She had a point there. He knew of some bungalows in Bandra, in Chembur and in Vashi. They either belonged to families that had been living for a very long time in the city or to wealthy people. Like businessmen, filmstars or politicians. *Not* corporate executives. There may be exceptions to this, but he knew her point had merit.

She continued, "Look at the road too, so beautiful, so clean. Don't think twice. Just go."

He smiled and shook his head again. "They need to select me first."

"Obviously, I am only talking about if they do. And I have a feeling they *will* select you."

"And how do you know this?" He asked her with a tinge of incredulity in his voice.

She smiled. "Did you go looking for a job in Zimbabwe?"

He shook his head. "I don't think *anybody* does."

"Exactly. They found you. They called you up. They interviewed you. These are signs that it's meant to be."

"Ok, ok, let's see. And there are still other things."

"Like what things?"

"Well, if I go there, I can't come back to India for work."

"Why so?"

"Ma, Africa is way behind in technology and systems. Once I have gone to Africa, I will need to keep working in Africa."

"OK and you will make more money too. So what's wrong with that?"

"And who will look after you? What will you do?"

"You said it will be a two year contract. Don't worry."

"Ma, that's what I am saying. After those two years, I will either continue in that company or find some other job but I will have to keep working in Africa. Pa will retire this year. You will get old."

She frowned. "I am *not* old."

"Ma, I am serious."

She smiled, "I am also serious. Do you think we want anything but the best for you? We will take care of ourselves. You go where your work takes you."

He shrugged. "It's not such an easy decision for me. I have lived here all my life. I haven't even worked outside Mumbai in all this time and now I am going to go all the way to Zimbabwe?"

"Who says you can't?"

"I can. At least I *think* so. But do I want to? I am not yet so sure."

Just as he was thinking through this, he got a call. It was from Rohan.

He had met Rohan at a FICCI meet that he had been asked to attend. Rohan was in his twenties and had moved to Mumbai for work from Ratnagiri. During their first meeting, Shailesh had mentioned something about catching a train from VT and Rohan had immediately corrected him with, "Chatrapati Shivaji Maharaj Terminus." Far from getting irritated, as many a long time Mumbaiite might have, Shailesh took a liking to Rohan and they had kept in touch.

He took the phone and said, "*Kasa kai?*" (Marathi greeting, equivalent to howdy)

"*Ekdum majet.*" Rohan said. (Again Marathi, a slangy equivalent to 'I am fine').

"What are you doing?"

"I am free today evening. Shall we meet?"

"Sure. Where do you have in mind?"

"There's a nice place my friends have recommended. Let's go there. I will send you the location."

"Cool. Where is it?"

"Powai."

"Ohhh."

"*Yaar*, I am in Andheri and you're in Mulund. Best meeting point is Powai. Nothing much to do in Ghatkopar."

"Fine, no problem. What time do you suggest?"

"Let's catch up around 8."

In order to reach the place by 8, Shailesh estimated he would have to start no later than 6.30. He would have to take a cab as the car had yet to recover from Tuesday's adventures.

Sure enough, at 6, when he checked the traffic on Maps, it indicated 90 minutes.

At 6:10, he started looking for rides.

The wait times were in the region of 10 minutes. And the ride would set him back by 700 bucks.

He grimaced and accepted, letting the aggregator process a ride for him.

After a couple of minutes, he got a call. The number suggested it was probably the driver of the vehicle that had been booked by the app.

"Sir, where do you want to go?" The driver asked.

"Powai." Shailesh replied.

"How much is it showing?"

"700."

"That is not enough. No use. So much traffic and just 700."

"What should I do? I won't cancel the ride. I will be charged for it."

"Ok, ok, I will cancel it." Said the driver angrily as he disconnected the call.

In another couple of minutes, the details of another driver appeared on the app screen. The wait time remained at 10 minutes. Which effectively meant the driver would now be here at 6.25 and not 6.20.

Once more, in a couple of minutes, the driver called and asked for the location.

Shailesh said Powai.

The driver simply noted it and disconnected the call. In an instant, the ride had been cancelled.

At the fourth time of asking, a driver finally accepted the ride. It was one Muhammad Wasim.

He had one request. He had heard the call for prayers just now and would take ten minutes to finish offering namaz.

Shailesh wasn't too chuffed about that but had no choice but to acquiesce. At least Muhammad had signed up for the ride.

10 minutes turned to 15. It was 6.45 when Muhammad finally came along to pick him up.

Before Shailesh could even start to upbraid him, Muhammad apologized sincerely for being late and promised to make amends.

Shailesh and Muhammad both knew keeping that promise required co-operation from the deity called

Mumbai traffic. But Shailesh appreciated the offer by Muhammad to make amends.

The EEH was relatively free and Muhammad looked on course to keep his promise as he sped through the Eastern suburbs. Even at the right turn to Jogeshwari Vikhroli Link Road (called JVLR colloquially), there wasn't the usual serpentine queue.

Right from Gandhi Nagar flyover, though, the infamous Powai crawl commenced.

A couple of Shailesh's college mates had gone way to Bengaluru for work. They often complained about the traffic there and cited Silk Board. To their Silk Board, he would raise a Powai every time. When he had once come across a news article discussing the traffic in Powai, he felt as if he had been vindicated. In his view, Powai could take on the worst traffic jams in the world and fight them to death. Maybe Silk Board v/s Powai would be like the Ali-Frazier bouts but at least that.

From Gandhi Nagar to IIT junction took a solid half an hour. Walking would be faster, but the place was tucked a long way in left from Hiranandani and on the hills. It was too far to walk. And there was hardly any space on the road to walk anyway.

Just as the cab crawled out of IIT, Rohan called. When Shailesh said he was getting out of IIT, Rohan was delighted and said he hoped to see him soon. Shailesh told him to order juice and starters and that he expected to be there in twenty minutes.

Muhammad partially made amends. He got to the place in fifteen minutes instead.

Shailesh offered to transfer via UPI, but Muhammad insisted on cash. This was one thing that puzzled him about Mumbai. On a recent visit to Chennai, he had found the autowalas insisting on UPI, saying it was convenient that way for them to transfer money to anybody they needed to make a payment to. In Mumbai, though, cash was still king. He remembered how during lockdowns, the *kirana* stores had started accepting online payments only to roll it right back the moment things returned to normal.

The exact fare was 702. Shailesh fumbled around and found 700. He didn't have the 2 rupees of change on him.

He said to Muhammad he didn't have 2 rupees. Muhammad said nothing but had a scowl on his face.

After a few moments of both staring at each other silently, Shailesh just walked off. It helped that there was a spot of rain just then that necessitated using the umbrella and getting a move-on.

Muhammad lingered on in his vehicle for a while, hoping to still get the 2 rupees owed him, before driving off.

He took the lift to head to the second floor where the restaurant was on a terrace. Pity they would have the sheets on because of the rain.

As he entered and tried to explain to the bouncer where he needed to go, Rohan waved and called out to him from a nearby table. Shailesh indicated to the bouncer that that's where he would sit and made off.

As the two exchanged warm greetings again, the waiter arrived with perfect timing to serve them a glass of mojito each.

Rohan beamed as he looked around the place and said, "It's really cool, isn't it? On an elevation."

Shailesh was so pensive in response he was slightly taken aback by himself. He said, "Well, I remember when Powai was just Hiranandani and these hills."

"Really?" Rohan asked with disbelief.

Shailesh nodded and flipped through his phone gallery. He had converted some of the old photos taken on analog to digital and had them on the phone.

He showed Rohan a photo of himself as a school child from the terrace of one of the skyscrapers in Hiranandani. He had gone there with parents when they had visited a family friend living in Hiranandani. Behind himself could be seen lush green hills, undisturbed by any trace of concrete. The photo could not capture it, but he could feel again the cool breeze that had enveloped him as he had stood happily for that photo.

Rohan observed the photo with surprise and then said, "Wow! They have developed Powai so much now. Unbelievable!"

Shailesh was incredulous. He gestured at the restaurant and said, "You call all this…development?"

Rohan was non-plussed. "What would you call it?"

"Rather than using big adjectives, I will use an objective and scientific term – deforestation."

Rohan laughed.

Shailesh was irritated. He said, "Don't laugh, Rohan. Powai was a green lung for the city, for the suburbs. Powai and the national park together provided relief from the congestion. The national park survives but Powai is gone."

Rohan was polite but persistent. "That is the price of development. When you look back, the old pictures will always look beautiful because you have memories associated with them."

Shailesh shook his head. "That's not what I mean at all. I have seen this city get concretized to an unprecedented level. Where every open space has been or is being sucked out. Either to make new buildings or to build flyovers."

"With all these flyovers, the traffic is so bad. Imagine what it would be without them."

"You wouldn't need so many flyovers if you didn't keep building so many skyscrapers."

"But what else to do, *yaar*. This is a huge city. What other purpose does it have? If Mumbai stops building, where will we go for jobs?"

"What do you mean?"

"Well, since you are so fond of greenery, you're most welcome to come and live in Ratnagiri. You will find all the greenery you want there. And no jobs. Why do you think I had to leave home and come all the way to Mumbai? Be practical, man."

"But Mumbai can't carry the load of the entire state of Maharashtra."

"That is an issue for the politicians to fix. Until then, we are happy that Mumbai keeps building and building. As long as Mumbai grows, there will be more jobs."

"But will it be liveable?"

"Don't we need a job first to be able to live?"

Shailesh looked at him for a minute in silence before he said, "You're right. And you have helped me make my mind. I must go then."

"Wait, wait, where are you going? Even the starters haven't come."

Shailesh laughed. "I didn't mean that way. I meant I must take the job and go out of Mumbai."

"To where?"

"Zimbabwe."

It was Rohan's turn to be incredulous. "What!"

Shailesh nodded. "The salary is very good. I will make 60% more compared to what I do here."

"But Zimbabwe."

Shailesh continued. "They will give me accommodation and transport. I have to spend only on food. So the savings potential is tremendous."

"But Zimbabwe."

"Well, you can have a look at these photos and see if you still want to say that."

He showed him the photos Mukesh had shared.

If Rohan was envious of what he saw, he didn't let on. He looked at it and then said, "I only want to live here in India. My *matrubhoomi* (motherland)."

"Nobody treats their mother the way we do this country." Shailesh quipped.

"You may be right. But still, I am not going anywhere. I am proud to be Indian."

"Hello, I am still Indian too. I will be going on a permit. Provided they make me an offer, of course."

"They will definitely make you an offer, man. You would have aced the interview. You're so smart."

"Isn't that a bit too much?"

Rohan shook his head. "You are. I respect you as a senior in our profession. I have learnt so much from you. If you do go, I will miss you."

Shailesh was touched. "I will miss you too, man. Let me know if you change your mind. There are plenty of accounts and finance jobs in Zimbabwe."

Rohan shook his head again and placed a hand on his heart.

After dinner, Shailesh booked another ride for the return trip.

As soon as he got into the cab, he called mother.

She took the call and immediately asked, "Have you started?"

"Yes ma."

"Good."

"Also…"

"Yes?"

"There is no need to discuss with pa."

"What do you mean?"

"I have decided. I am very clear in my mind now."

"I am not following."

"I am going to Zimbabwe." He declared.

"Ohhh…" As she understood.

"All the best, da."

"They need to offer me the job."

"Yes, yes, this is a contingent all the best."

Shailesh laughed.

She added, "Remember, I studied accounting too."

8ᵗʰ *September*

"Zimbabwe?"

Shailesh's friends were incredulous.

Yesterday night, he had announced on 'College Masti' that he was going to Zimbabwe. Vineet and Ashutosh had immediately demanded to meet. But Pradeep and Sumedh had begged off, saying they had already made plans. So, instead, the band of five had scheduled a Zoom call for the morning.

And the first thing they wanted to know was, "(Why) Zimbabwe?"

Met with this reaction of surprise, he played down his chances. "They need to make me an offer first."

Vineeth said. "They will definitely make you an offer, man. Who's going to go to Zimbabwe?"

Shailesh replied, "Well, they tell me they already have twenty Indians working there."

"Is it?" Vineeth appeared to be even more surprised.

"Will they provide accommodation?" Pradeep asked.

Shailesh said yes and shared the photos.

"Wow." Pradeep whistled.

Ashutosh still expressed scepticism. "Man, Africa is unpredictable, all said and done. Have you read about what happened in the 2000s in Zimbabwe?"

Shailesh replied, "Yes, I have. I have a distant relative in Zambia. So, through him, I have enquired and the situation has been stable for many years."

"It was stable before the 2000s too." Ashutosh said.

"Look, I have to take a chance." Shailesh reasoned.

"But why?" Ashutosh persisted. "If you want growth, you could just look for a good opening here."

"Well…" Shailesh paused as he searched for the words.

He ventured. "Well, maybe Zimbabwe looks riskier but at least while things are ok there, I will get to enjoy a car pick up and drop and escape from the trains."

"You can do that here too. You drive to work once in a while, don't you? Sumedh pointed out.

"I do. And it can take me up to two hours on bad days."

"It won't in Zimbabwe?"

Shailesh shook his head. "They said just twenty minutes."

"They may be lying."

"Well, I asked around and it's true. There's not much traffic in Harare. Just check out the population. It's nothing like Mumbai."

He added, "And also, because of the low population, pollution is low too."

"And you know this, how?"

"I checked the AQI reading for Harare online."

"They could be lying."

Shailesh was getting a little exasperated. "Well, not as if Mumbai is exactly a bastion of transparency."

Vineet interjected. "Dude, why do you hate India so much?"

Shailesh shrugged. "I wouldn't call it hate."

"Then?"

"Well, do I have to hate India to be open to working in Harare? Besides, I am talking about Mumbai. I haven't..."

"Worked or lived anywhere else." Pradeep interjected. "And now you are going to work somewhere in Africa?"

Shailesh laughed. "Well, I just didn't try hard enough all this time to get a job elsewhere in India. It's not as if I was looking for this one either. I just got the call."

"So...now that you have opened your mind to the possibility of working in Africa, why not just look for a job in India?"

"I could…."

"Yes, and what's stopping you?" Ashutosh asked.

"I *think* the problems will be roughly similar to what we already have in Mumbai."

"Do you think there won't be *any* problems in Zimbabwe?"

"No, I am quite sure there will be problems. Plenty of them."

"In that case?"

"I am also equally sure these will be a very different set of problems."

"So you're tired of which problems, exactly?" Sumedh jumped back in.

"I told you already. Traffic, pollution, lack of cleanliness, overcrowding, pushing-and-shoving, general rudeness, corporates insisting on long hours and working from office even when most of us have long commutes."

"Shailesh, don't mistake me, I am not trying to get personal. Just playing devil's advocate. Have you never pushed around at railway stations or in trains?" Ashutosh again.

"I have, no denying. To survive in this ecosystem, you must do all those things. Can I be different in a different ecosystem? I would like to find out. Can I not live without doing side-please all the time?"

"But…Zimbabwe?" Pradeep wasn't done just yet.

Shailesh started to lose his patience. "Well, it's not like I have an offer from some European country. I need to work with what I've got. And, again, I don't have an offer yet for Zimbabwe for that matter."

"You were trying for Australia, no?" Vineet remembered, not very helpfully.

"Yes, and after four attempts, I gave up trying to ace PTE."

"You told me about it, I remember. But Shailesh, just because you couldn't clear it doesn't necessarily mean it's rigged."

"Who cares. I can't go on trying. And another thing. I'll have to go and look for a job *after* landing up there. Burning through savings in the meantime.

This job is going to add to my savings from day one. And at twice the rate as my current rate of savings."

"Obviously, they're paying you that much because it's that tough to survive there." Ashutosh continued to sow the seeds of doubt.

"Or, they just need talent. Or maybe, being an Indian company, they want to have Indians in managerial positions. Could be just a control issue. That's what my uncle was telling me. It's usually just about control. And plus, we will slog. They won't."

"So there also you will have to slog only, na?"

"Yes. But I won't have to spend minimum three hours two way on the commute after that."

It was Sumedh's turn to express exasperation. "I don't get it, man. You did it all this time. You have been comfortable with the commute for so long."

"Doesn't mean I *love* it. Tell me, do you honestly *love* sitting in traffic or getting crushed in the trains?"

"No."

"And if *you* had an opportunity to work…"

Sumedh cut him off. "Dude, I love Mumbai. I can't imagine living anywhere else."

"Seriously?" Shailesh's turn to be incredulous.

"Yup, dead serious." Sumedh said with a smile.

"Why?"

"What do you mean why? Is love supposed to be rational? I just love it, that's all. No reasons needed."

"Ah, ok, so you admit you can't justify it."

"More like, I don't *need* to, I don't *have* to. I just can't imagine living anywhere else."

"You've been to New York, haven't you?" Shailesh asked.

"More often than you have."

"And you'd still say that?"

Sumedh nodded. "Mumbai is in my bloodstream, man."

Shailesh shrugged. "Good for you."

Vineet was curious. "You know, I am sure I remember you telling someone else once that you couldn't imagine living anywhere else."

Shailesh shrugged again, "Something changed, I guess."

* * *

He thought about it as he booked a cab ride to the airport. Father's trip had been ten days long, so he had taken along two travel bags. Shailesh was going over to help with the baggage.

Something had indeed changed. Had it really only changed over this week or had the feeling simply manifested itself strongly for the first time now?

But it was only lately he had realized how much he had come to dislike living in Mumbai.

And Vineet was right. This didn't make sense at one level. He had lived here all these years. This was the only city he had known. None of the things he was complaining about were new. So why now?

As he was pondering over this, it took him a while to hear his father calling out to him.

He walked over to where the latter was.

Father greeted him, "Shailesh!"

Shailesh took up a very upright posture and said, "Sir!" He did eschew the salute, though.

Father chuckled and patted him on the shoulder.

"How are you da?" He hugged Shailesh tightly.

"I am ok, pa." Shailesh said, as he helped push the bags to the pickup point where the cabbie then loaded them in the boot.

As they settled in for the ride, father asked, "So… how did the interview go?"

"Very well."

"Good! So now you need to decide."

"I have already decided."

"What? Don't make any hasty decision. Don't dismiss.."

Shailesh said, "I have decided to go to Zimbabwe if they make me an offer."

Father whistled. "Oh! Big move, huh."

"Yeah, it will be a good change."

Father rephrased it slightly, "It will be a change, that's true."

"Less traffic, less pollution, those are things to look forward to."

"True but there will be other things. Prepare yourself mentally for it."

Shailesh nodded vigorously.

He then added, "I am just fed up of Mumbai, so I will embrace a change with open arms."

Father replied, "That's good but remember you weren't even applying for opportunities. Not even for jobs in other cities in India. So maybe you weren't so fed up that you wanted to change your location ASAP. Sumitra tells me that you weren't even super eager for this Zimbabwe opportunity and she had to encourage you. So maybe you're making up a narrative to rationalize the risk you are taking? I don't know, think about it."

Shailesh fell silent.

Father added, "I just want to say one thing. If you're going in the spirit of adventure, it's good. It's the right time to take such risks. But don't go because you want to run away from Ajay sir."

9th September

Ajay walked into the office. Or rather, stormed in. When he returned from a leave, he usually felt extra charged up, filled with even more passion than before. The passion was usually, and unfortunately, directed to his reportees. Watching the spring in his step, Kunal shuddered. He looked around nervously. There was no sign of Shailesh.

Ajay sat down, placed his bag down by the desk and dialled Shailesh's extension. There was no answer.

He stormed out of his cabin now and marched towards Kunal.

"Where is he?" He demanded to know.

Kunal was too smart, too well versed in managing Ajay to ask who. He simply intoned a doubtful, "Sir?"

"That dude. Shailesh. Where is he?"

Kunal shrugged. "Don't know sir. No message from him."

"But it's 10."

"Yes sir."

"What yes sir? Why haven't you found out?"

"Sir, I called him. He didn't pick up."

For a second, Kunal feared Ajay would ask to look at his phone.

Instead, Ajay pulled out his own phone from the pocket and called Shailesh's number. Kunal could breathe easy.

After several rings, the call wasn't answered. Ajay's fury escalated.

He fumed, "I will call HR and ask them to issue him a warning letter. Is late to work, doesn't inform anyone, doesn't pick up calls…"

Just as he was saying all this, Shailesh walked into the office.

Ajay paused and took in what he was seeing. There was nothing different about Shailesh, on the surface. And yet, something just felt different. The glow on his face, the relaxed posture, his leisurely walking pace. Yes, there was an air of nonchalance about him that Ajay hadn't observed before.

Shailesh looked Ajay firmly in the eye with a confidence that the latter found disconcerting.

Looking at his phone, he said, "Sir, you were looking for me?"

Ajay barked, "What do you mean, looking for you? Of course I am looking for you. You're late. You didn't pick up my call. You didn't inform your colleague. And when he…"

Just as Kunal feared his cover was about to be blown, Shailesh spoke up, "Sir, I have something to discuss for which this (gesturing at the open cubicle area) might not be the best place."

Ajay said, still angrily, "Alright, come into my cabin."

Ajay stormed back in while Shailesh followed behind at his own leisurely pace.

This nonchalance didn't sit well with Ajay and he fumed again, "This attitude of yours is going to get you in trouble."

"Good for me then that I am resigning today." Shailesh dropped the bomb as gently as a mother sliding her baby into a cradle.

Ajay's eyes nearly fell out from their sockets.

"What!" He exclaimed.

Shailesh nodded. "I've got a better opportunity and am interested in pursuing it."

"But….but…" Ajay began to stutter in panic. "Who will do…"

Shailesh shook his head and shrugged. "I am afraid you will have to find a replacement or reorganize the work within the team."

Ajay nodded gruffly and said, "You have to serve out your notice period."

"I am afraid sir that I will have to leave in 1.5 months."

"Who gave you permission to leave half a month early? I won't allow it."

Shailesh shrugged. "Sir, it is your choice. But it is my duty to notify you of my last day so that you can plan, so that you are not looking for me after 1.5 months are over."

Ajay angrily shook his head. "So much attitude. Listen, I am going to screw you. I won't give you relieving. Enough is enough."

It was all Shailesh could do to suppress a chuckle. "I am sorry to inform you that I won't need a relieving letter."

Ajay was incredulous. "What!"

"My next job is in Africa and nobody asks for relieving letters there."

"Obviously…if you go to that kind of country." Ajay was disdainful.

"Sir, that is my choice. I have decided. Would you like to come too?"

Ajay glared at him. He yelled, "Out. Out of my office before I kill you."

* * *

At 5, Shailesh turned off his laptop, packed his bag, took one glance at Ajay (who immediately gestured as if to ask how this was allowed) and walked out.

As he was walking out, he met Mansi in the corridor.

"Hi handsome." She greeted him, making him blush.

She asked, "Is it true what the grapevine's telling me about you?"

He nodded.

"Hmmm. You don't need to tell me which company but…Mumbai or some other city?"

"It's actually Harare, the capital of Zimbabwe."

"Ohhh!" She exclaimed in surprise.

She asked, "Africa, right?"

He nodded in confirmation.

As the news sank in, she said, "So…because you couldn't change your reality, you changed the reality itself?"

Bemused, he said, "That's one way of putting it."

She shrugged and said, "I hope you'll find there what you've been looking for."

He replied, "I hope so too."

"Going home?"

After a lengthy pause, he said he was.

She raised her eyebrows quizzically.

As she was about to move on, he remembered something and called out, "Ma'am?"

"Yes?" She turned around and asked.

"That rock lover boyfriend of yours…was his name Melvin?"

Her face went pale in an instant. Rather tersely, she said, "Are you sure that's not too much information?"

He bit his lips, nodded, turned around and went on his way without looking back.

He had somewhere to go before he went home. But it wouldn't be Marine Drive this time.

He took the 310 to Kurla station. But upon reaching Kurla, he took a train to CSMT instead of a North-bound train.

He got down at the very next station, Sion.

From there, he crossed the road and proceeded in the direction of the old SIES college.

Nearby was a shop called Guru Kripa.

It wasn't particularly well known across the city, but it was world famous in Sion-Matunga.

The band of five had visited it too many times to be able to keep track of.

It was renowned for its *samosa-ragda*. Spicy as hell but fresh and delicious.

As he had expected, it was super-crowded.

He had to wait quite a while to get *his* plate.

But as he bit into the *samosa*, any lingering irritation over the wait disappeared.

The wait had been more than worth it.

His friends weren't around. Had they had their meet at Gurukripa and not on Zoom yesterday, the conversation would likely have been very different. No matter. As he chewed on the samosa, he could feel their arms on his shoulders, he could hear their laughter and see their toothy grins.

It wasn't just a stately and timeless monument. Even a humble samosa held so many memories. And these memories were priceless. Certainly a lot more expensive than the modest charge Gurukripa commanded for the samosa-ragda.

And there was no branch of Gurukripa outside Sion. Which meant there certainly wouldn't be one in Harare.

Man, he had already resigned and rather gleefully at that. Was this really going to work? It had better. The deed had been done. He had said yes.

He asked them to pack a parcel for him. If he wasn't going to be able to visit Gurukripa for a long time, he could at least feast on their offerings to his heart's content while he could.

He picked up the parcel, placed neatly in a plastic bag that bore their name, and walked towards Sion station.

He got into the train, holding the parcel tight, covering it with both hands in a desperate bid to protect it from the attack of the commuters.

Other commuters curiously eyed the package. And then, they smelt the aroma of the hot *samosa* and curiosity turned to longing. They looked on wistfully even as Shailesh continued to protect the package with all his might.

Post Script

A month later

Shailesh looked at his watch. It was 6. The car was supposed to arrive any minute. No, his car was in the pink of health. But today, he wouldn't be returning home from the ride. He was flying and on a one way ticket at that.

The day had arrived. The day he would fly out to Zimbabwe. He had to pinch himself to believe this wasn't a dream, that this was happening. This still seemed to him like a selection of the unlikeliest of possibilities that had somehow conspired to happen to him. He was excited but also…anxious. And a little scared.

He had wrestled all this time with the question. And as the moment neared, so too the trepidation multiplied manifold. How would he cope with leaving Mumbai? For better or worse, it was the only city he had lived in from…the day he was born?

Unlike some other Mumbaiites, he hadn't even left the city in the womb of his mother for her to be with her parents. He had been born in a Mumbai hospital. He had studied in Mumbai. He had worked all this time in Mumbai. He had spent more days than he could remember hanging out at Marine Drive.

And now…he was leaving it all behind for… Zimbabwe? Where he would be making a lot more money, yes, but where life was, from what he had gathered, ten years behind India, it not more. Wouldn't he be regressing in his career too by signing up for this? And would there even be an option to work in India again? In the zoom call, his friends had indeed warned him that finding work in India would be all but impossible once he had spent more than a year in Africa. Something he had already suspected even before he had accepted the offer.

And here he was, signing up for something that had so many elements of the unknown…with the only known element being that it was potentially a death warrant for the career he had built up to that point in India.

Something about this didn't seem to make sense. But if this was so, it was possibly too late to make amends. The one-way ticket to Harare that his would-be employer had purchased for him stared at him and said hi. He returned the greeting doubtfully.

As he processed this sense of unease, the sound of a car horn brought him back to the here-and-now. It was here. It was time.

He hugged his parents tightly. They would be accompanying him to the airport. Nevertheless, the emotions had already started to rise up to the surface. He could hardly contain himself.

He pushed two giant travel bags into the elevator. They were carefully spec-ed to fit within millimetres of the airline's permissible dimensions for check-in-bags. He wore a backpack which had a spare laptop and some books. He had no idea what to expect from Zimbabwe…and he certainly didn't want to get bored there!

He greeted the car driver. They hired this car whenever Shailesh's aunt and uncle from Australia came over.

Shailesh's father proudly told the driver, "Today, he is going to take the flight." And pointed to Shailesh.

Shailesh was embarrassed. "Pa, I am only going to Zimbabwe, not somewhere in Europe."

"It's an adventure. And besides, you're going to make good money. More than you were making here."

True enough on both counts, he reasoned. It pushed the fears a little to the back of his mind. He had much to look forward to. But a voice in his head insisted there would be stuff he hadn't bargained for.

Oh well, it was too late to not board the flight now!

He and his parents got in the car. The driver confirmed that it was good to go and vroomed into action.

Soon enough, he turned left from LBS onto the road leading to the Nahur bridge that crossed the railway tracks, leading onwards to the EEH.

As the car climbed the bridge, a CSMT-bound local train passed underneath on the tracks.

By the looks of it, it was packed. He could see myriad heads bobbing out of the doors. Yes, some of them simply wanted to catch the breeze. But he knew from experience of travelling every day by train that the trains simply were already crowded. It wasn't even past 6.30 and already, anybody trying to get in after Mulund would find themselves having to stand…and not very comfortably at that. The peak hour crush had already begun.

And that's when it came to him. Yes, this is what he was leaving behind. Whatever else he would or wouldn't have to do in Zimbabwe, he knew for sure he wouldn't have to endure travelling by jam-packed trains, where the crowds crushed your bones. He wouldn't be bathed in sweat, his hair wouldn't be dishevelled and, most importantly, he wouldn't be feeling tired even by the time he was stepping into office.

Heck, *if* moving to Zimbabwe for work meant no longer having to travel by local trains that were crowded almost irrespective of the time of day, it maybe wasn't *such* a bad thing after all.

And *maybe*, incredible as it sounded, he wouldn't miss Mumbai very much. *Maybe.*